In a definitive series of articles
about Rex Stout and his monumental
creation, NERO WOLFE,
The New Yorker once remarked: "Nero Wolfe, the fat
sedentary detective, invented by Rex Stout, is an
interesting fellow because the author is an
interesting fellow."

Nero Wolfe owes his knowledge of practically everything
to the amazing background of his creator
who has been, among other things:
banker, barker, bookworm, bookkeeper, yeoman
on the Presidential yacht, boss of three thousand
propaganda writers in World War II, gentleman farmer,
big businessman, cigar salesman, pueblo guide, hotel
manager, architect, cabinet-maker, crow trainer,
jumping-pig trainer, mammoth-pumpkin grower, politician,
potted-plant wizard, gastronome, president of the
Authors' Guild, usher, ostler, and pamphleteer.

Rex Stout is also one of the best mystery writers who ever
lived, and Nero Wolfe is one of fiction's truly great
detectives. TRIPLE JEOPARDY is up to their standard.

Books by Rex Stout

THE SILENT SPEAKER
TOO MANY WOMEN
AND BE A VILLAIN
TROUBLE IN TRIPLICATE
MURDER BY THE BOOK
TRIPLE JEOPARDY
PRISONER'S BASE
THE GOLDEN SPIDERS
THREE MEN OUT
THE BLACK MOUNTAIN
BEFORE MIDNIGHT
THREE WITNESSES
MIGHT AS WELL BE DEAD
THREE FOR THE CHAIR
IF DEATH EVER SLEPT
AND FOUR TO GO
CHAMPAGNE FOR ONE
PLOT IT YOURSELF
THE SECOND CONFESSION
THREE AT WOLFE'S DOOR
TOO MANY CLIENTS
IN THE BEST FAMILIES
THE FINAL DEDUCTION

Published by Bantam Books

A NERO WOLFE THREESOME

TRIPLE JEOPARDY

BY REX STOUT

*This low-priced Bantam Book
has been completely reset in a type face
designed for easy reading, and was
printed from new plates. It contains the complete
text of the original hard-cover edition.*
NOT ONE WORD HAS BEEN OMITTED.

🐦

TRIPLE JEOPARDY
*A Bantam Book / published by arrangement with
The Viking Press, Inc.*

PRINTING HISTORY
*Viking edition published March 1952
Dollar Mystery Guild edition published July 1952*
Acknowledgment is made to the AMERICAN MAGAZINE, in
*which these short novels originally appeared in 1951-1952.
The magazine title for "The Squirt and the Monkey" was
"See No Evil"; for "Home to Roost," "Nero Wolfe and the
Communist Killer."*
*Bantam edition published July 1957
2nd printing .....August 1957
3rd printing ....July 1963
4th printing*

ISBN 978-0-553-76307-2

*Bantam Books are published by Bantam Books, Inc. Its trade-mark,
consisting of the words "Bantam Books" and the portrayal of a
bantam, is registered in the United States Patent Office and in other
countries. Marca Registrada. Printed in the United States of America. Bantam Books, Inc., 271 Madison Ave., New York 16, N. Y.*

147028622

Contents

HOME TO ROOST

I

"**O**UR nephew Arthur was the romantic type," said Mrs. Benjamin Rackell with the least possible movement of her thin tight lips. "He thought being a Communist was romantic."

Nero Wolfe, behind his desk in his outsized chair that thought nothing of his seventh of a ton, scowled at her. I, at my own desk with a notebook and pen, permitted myself a private grin, not unsympathetic. Wolfe was controlling himself under severe provocation. The appointment for Mr. Rackell to call at Wolfe's office on the ground floor of his old brownstone house on West Thirty-fifth Street, at six p.m., had been made by phone by a secretary in the office of the Rackell Importing Company, and nothing had been said about a wife coming along. And the wife, no treat as a spectacle to begin with, was an interrupter and a cliché tosser, enough to make Wolfe scowl at any man, let alone a woman.

"But," he objected, not too caustic, "you say that he was not a Communist, that, on the contrary, he was acting for the FBI when he joined the Communist party."

He would have loved to tell her to get lost. But his house had five stories, counting the basement and the plant rooms full of orchids on the roof, and there was Fritz the chef and Theodore the botanist and me, Archie Goodwin,

1

the fairly confidential assistant, with nothing to carry the load but his income as a private detective; and the Rackell check for three thousand bucks, offered as a retainer, was under a paperweight on his desk.

"That's just it," Mrs. Rackell said impatiently. "Isn't it romantic to work for the FBI? But that wasn't why he did it; he did it to serve his country, and that's why they killed him. His being the romantic type had nothing to do with it."

Wolfe made a face and undertook to bypass her. His eyes went to Rackell. She would probably have called her husband the stubby type, with his short arms and legs, but he was no runt. His trunk was long and broad and his head long and narrow. His eyes pointed down at the corners, and so did his mouth, making him look mournful.

Wolfe asked him, "Have you spoken with the FBI, Mr. Rackell?"

But the wife answered. "No, he hasn't," she said. "I went myself yesterday, and I never heard anything to equal it. They wouldn't tell me a single thing. They wouldn't even admit Arthur was working for them as a spy for his country! They said it was a matter for the New York police and I should talk to them—as if I hadn't!"

"I told you, Pauline," Rackell said mildly but not timidly, "that the FBI won't tell people things. And the police won't either, not when it's murder, and especially when the Communists come into it. That's why I insisted on coming to Nero Wolfe to find out what's going on. If the FBI doesn't want it known that Arthur was with them, even if it means not getting his murderer, what else can you expect?"

"I expect justice!" Mrs. Rackell declared, her lips actually moving visibly.

I gave it a line to itself in the notebook.

Wolfe was frowning at Rackell. "There seems to be some confusion. I understood that you want a murder investigated. Now you say you came to me to find out what's going on. If you mean you want me to investigate the police and the FBI, that's too big a bite."

"I didn't say that," Rackell protested.

"No, but clear it up. What do you want?"

Rackell's down-pointing eyes looked even mournfuller. "We want facts," he declared. "I think the police and the FBI are quite capable of sacrificing the rights of a private citizen to what they consider the public interest. Our nephew was murdered, and my wife had a right to ask them what line they're proceeding on, and they wouldn't tell her. I don't intend to just let it go at that. Is this a democracy or isn't it? I'm not—"

"No!" the wife snapped. "It's not a democracy, it's a republic."

"I suggest," said Wolfe, exasperated, "that I recapitulate to see if I have it straight. I'll combine what I have read in the papers with what you have told me." He focused on the wife, probably figuring that she would be less apt to cut in if he held her eye. "Arthur Rackell, your husband's orphaned nephew, was a fairly efficient employee of his importing business, drawing a good salary, living at your home here in New York, on Sixty-eighth Street. Some three years ago you noted that he was taking a radically leftist position in discussions of political and social questions, and you remonstrated without effect. As time passed he became more leftist and more outspoken, until his opinions and arguments were identical with the Communist line. You, both you and your husband, argued with him and entreated him, but—"

"I did," Mrs. Rackell snapped. "My husband didn't."

"Now, Pauline," Rackell protested. "I argued with him some." He looked at Wolfe. "I didn't entreat him because I didn't think I had a right to. I don't believe in entreating people about their convictions. I was paying him a salary and I didn't want him to think he had to—" The importer fluttered a hand. "I liked Arthur, and he was my brother's son."

"In any case," Wolfe went on brusquely, still at the wife, "he did not change. He stubbornly adhered to the Communist position. He applauded the Communist attack in Korea and denounced the action of the United Nations. You finally found it insufferable and gave him an ultimatum: either he would abandon his outrageous—"

"Not an ultimatum," Mrs. Rackell corrected. "My husband refused to permit it. I merely—"

Wolfe outspoke her. "At least you made it plain that you had had enough and he was no longer welcome in your home. You must have made it fairly strong, since he was moved to disclose an extremely tight secret: that he had been persuaded by the FBI, back in nineteen forty-eight, to join the Communist party for the purpose of espionage. No easy admonition would have dragged that out of him, surely."

"I didn't say it was easy. I told him—" She stopped, and the thin lips really did tighten. She relaxed them enough to let words out. "I think he thought he would lose his job, and he was well paid. Much more than he earned, the amount of work he did."

Wolfe nodded. "Anyhow, he told you his secret, and you promised to keep it, becoming a confederate. Privately admiring him, with others you had to pretend to maintain your condemnation. You told your husband and no one else. That was about a week ago, you say?"

"Yes."

"And Saturday evening, three days ago, your nephew was murdered. Now to that. You have added little to what the papers have carried, but let's see. He left the apartment, your home, and took a taxi to Chezar's restaurant, where he had a dinner engagement. He had invited three women and two men to dine with him, and they were all there when he arrived, in the bar. When your nephew came they went with him to the table he had reserved and had cocktails. He took a small metal box from—"

"Gold."

"Gold is a metal, madam. He took it from a pocket, his side coat pocket, put it on the table, and left it there while he conferred with the waiter. There was conversation. When plates and rolls and butter were brought, the pillbox got pushed around. It was on the table altogether some ten or twelve minutes. When hors d'oeuvres were served, your nephew started to eat, remembered the pillbox, found it behind the basket of rolls, got from it a vitamin capsule, swallowed the capsule with a sip of water, and began on his hors d'oeuvres. Six or seven minutes later he suddenly cried out, sprang to his feet, overturning his chair, made convulsive gestures, became rigid, collapsed and crumpled to the floor, and died. A doctor arrived shortly, but he was already dead. It has been found that two other capsules in the metal box, similar in appearance to the one he took, contained what they were supposed to and were harmless; but your nephew had swallowed potassium cyanide. He was murdered by replacing a vitamin capsule with a capsule filled with poison."

"Certainly. That's what—"

"I'll go on, please. You were and are convinced that the substitution was made by one of his dinner companions who is a Communist and who learned that your nephew was acting for the FBI, and you so informed Inspector Cramer of the police. You were not satisfied with his acceptance of that information, especially in a subsequent talk with him yesterday morning, Monday, and went yourself to the office of the FBI, saw a Mr. Anstrey, and found him noncommittal. He took the position that a homicide in Manhattan is the business of the New York police. Exasperated, you went to Inspector Cramer's office, were unable to see him, talked with a sergeant named Stebbins, came away further exasperated, regarded with favor your husband's suggestion, made this morning, that I be consulted, and here you are. Have I left out anything important?"

"One little point." Rackell cleared his throat. "Our telling Inspector Cramer about Arthur's joining the Communist party for the FBI—that was in confidence. Of course this talk with you is confidential too, naturally, since we're your clients."

Wolfe shook his head. "Not yet. You want to hire me to investigate the death of your nephew?"

"Yes. Certainly."

"Then you should know that while no one excels me in discretion I will not work under restrictions."

"That's fair enough."

"Good. I'll let you know tomorrow, probably by noon." Wolfe reached to push the paperweight aside and pick up the check. "Shall I keep this meanwhile and return it if I can't take the job?"

Rackell frowned, perplexed. His wife snapped, "Why on earth couldn't you take it?"

"I don't know, madam. I hope to. I need the money. But I'll have to look into it a little—discreetly, of course. I'll let you know tomorrow at the latest." He extended a hand with the check. "Unless you prefer to take this and try elsewhere."

They didn't like it, especially her. She even left the red leather chair to take the check, her lips tight, but after some give-and-take with her husband they decided to let it ride, and she put the check back on the desk. They wanted to give us more details, especially about their nephew's five dinner guests, but Wolfe said that could wait, and they left, none too pleased. As I let them out at the front door Rackell gave me a polite thank-you nod, but she didn't even know I was there.

Returning to the office, I got the check and put it in the safe and then stood to regard Wolfe. His nose was twitching. He looked as if he had an oyster with horseradish on it in his mouth, a combination he detests.

"It can't be helped," I told him. "It takes all kinds to make a clientele. What are we going to look into a little?"

He sighed. "Get Mr. Wengert of the FBI. You want to see him, this evening if possible. I'll talk."

"It's nearly seven o'clock."

"Try."

I went to the phone on my desk, dialed RE 2-3500, talked to a stranger and to a man I had met a couple of times, and reported to Wolfe, "Not available. Tomorrow morning."

"Make an appointment."

I did so and hung up.

Wolfe sat scowling at me. He spoke. "I'll give you instructions after dinner. Have we got the *Gazette* of the past three days?"

"Sure."

"Let me have them, please. Confound it." He sighed again. "Saturday, and tomorrow's Wednesday. Like a warmed-over meal." He came erect and his face brightened. "I wonder how Fritz is making out with that fish." He left his chair and headed for the hall and the kitchen.

II

WEDNESDAY morning all the air in Manhattan was conditioned—the wrong way. It was no place for penguins. On my way to Foley Square my jacket was beside me on the seat of the taxi, but when I had paid the driver and got out I put it on. Sweat or no sweat, I had to show the world that a private detective can be tough enough to take it.

When, after some waiting, I got admitted to Wengert's big corner room I found him in his shirt sleeves with his tie and collar loosened. He got up to shake hands and invited me to sit. We exchanged remarks.

"I haven't seen you," I told him, "since you got elevated here. Congratulations."

"Thanks."

"You're welcome. I notice you've got brass in your voice, but I guess that can't be helped. Mr. Wolfe sends his regards."

"Give him mine." His voice warmed up a little, just perceptibly. "I'll never forget how he came through on that mercury thing." He glanced at the watch on his wrist. "What can I do for you, Goodwin?"

Back a few years, when we had been in G2 together, it had been Archie, but then he hadn't had a corner room with five phones on his desk. I crossed my legs to show there was no rush.

"Not a thing," I told him. "Mr. Wolfe just wants to clear. Yesterday a man and wife named Rackell came to see him. They want him to investigate the death of their nephew, Arthur Rackell. Do you know about it, or do you

want to call someone in? Mrs. Rackell has talked with a
Mr. Anstrey."

"I know. Go ahead."

"Then I won't have to draw pictures. Our bank says that
Rackell rates seven figures west of the decimal point, and
we would like to earn a fee by tagging a murderer, but our
country right or wrong. We would hate to torpedo the
ship of state in this bad weather. The Rackells came to Mr.
Wolfe because they think the FBI and the NYPD regard
the death of Arthur as a regrettable but minor incident.
They say he was killed by a Commie who discovered that
he was an FBI plant. Before we proceed on that theory Mr.
Wolfe wants to clear with you. Of course you may not want
to say, even under the rug to us, that he was yours. May
you?"

"It's hotter than yesterday," Wengert stated.

"Yeah. Would you care to make any sign at all, for instance a wink?"

"No."

"Then I'll try something more general. There has been
nothing in the papers about the Commie angle, not a
word, so there has been no mention of the FBI. Is the FBI
working on the murder, officially or otherwise?"

"Much hotter," he said.

"It sure is. How about the others, the five dinner guests?
Of course they're our meat. Any suggestions, requests, or
orders? Any strings you wouldn't want us to trip on?"

"The humidity, too."

"Absolutely. I realize that you would like to tell us to lay
off on general principles, but you're afraid there might be a
headline tomorrow, FBI WARNS NERO WOLFE TO KEEP HANDS
OFF OF RACKELL MURDER. Besides, if you give us a stop sign
you'll have to say why or we'll keep going. Just to clean it
up, it there any question I might ask that would take your
mind off the weather?"

"No." He stood up. "It was nice to see you for old time's
sake, and you can still give Wolfe my regards, but tell him
to go climb a tree. Some nerve. Sending you here with that
bull about wanting to clear! Why didn't he ask me to send
him up the files? Come again when I'm not here."

I was on my way, but before I reached the door I turned. "The radio said this morning it would hit ninety-five," I told him and went.

There are always taxis at Foley Square. I removed my jacket, climbed into one, and gave an address on West Twentieth Street. When we got there my shirt was stuck to the back of the seat. I pulled loose, paid, got out, put on the jacket, and went into a building. The headquarters of the Homicide Squad, Manhattan West, was much more familiar to me than the United States Courthouse. So were the inmates, one in particular, the one sitting at a dingy little desk in a dingy little room to which I was escorted. They have never let me roam loose in that building since the day I took a snapshot of a piece of paper they were saving, though they couldn't prove it.

Sergeant Purley Stebbins was big and strong but not handsome. His rusty old swivel chair squeaked and groaned as he leaned back.

"Oh, hell," I said, sitting, "I forgot. I meant to bring a can of oil for that chair my next trip here." I cocked my head. "What are you glaring about? Is my face dirty?"

"It don't have to be dirty." He went on glaring. "Goddam it, why did they have to pick Nero Wolfe?"

I considered a moment, maybe two seconds. "I am glad to know," I said pleasantly, "that the cops and the feds are collaborating so closely. Citizens can sleep sound. Wengert must have phoned the minute I left. What did he say?"

"He spoke to the Inspector. What do you want?"

"Maybe I should speak to the Inspector."

"He's busy. So the Rackells have hired Wolfe?"

I lifted my nose. "Mr. and Mrs. Rackell have asked Mr. Wolfe to investigate the death of their nephew. Before he starts to whiz through it like a cyclone he wants to know whether he will be cramping the style of those responsible for the national security. I've seen Wengert, and the heat has got him. He's not interested. I am now seeing you because of the Commie angle, which has not appeared in the papers. If it is against the public interest for us to take the job, tell me why. I know you and Cramer think it's against the public interest for us to eat, let alone detect, but that's not enough. We would need facts."

"Uh-huh," Purley growled. "We give 'em to you and Wolfe decides he can use 'em better than we can. Nuts. I'll tell you one fact: this one has got stingers. Lay off."

I nodded sympathetically. "That's probably good advice. I'll tell Mr. Wolfe." I arose. "We would like you to sign a statement covering the substance of this interview. Three copies, one—"

"Go somewhere," he rasped. "On out. Beat it."

I thought he was getting careless, but my escort, a paunchy old veteran with a pushed-in nose, was waiting in the hall. As I strode to the front and the entrance he waddled along behind.

It was past eleven by the time I got back to the office, so Wolfe had finished his two hours in the plant rooms and was behind his desk, with beer. It would have been impossible for anything with life in it to look less like a cyclone.

"Well?" he muttered at me.

I sat. "We deposit the check. Wengert sends his regards. Purley doesn't. They both think you sent me merely to get the dope for free and they sneer at the idea of our caring for the public welfare. Wengert phoned Cramer the minute I left. Not a peep from either one. We only know what we see in the papers."

He grunted. "Get Mr. Rackell."

So we had a case.

III

THERE were two open questions about the seven people gathered in the office after dinner that Wednesday evening: were any of them Commies, and was one of them a murderer? I make it seven, including our clients, not to seem prejudiced.

I had given them the eye as they arrived and gathered and now, as I sat at my desk with them all in sight, I was placing no bets. There had been a time, years back, when I had had the notion that no murderer, man or woman, could stand exposed to view and not let it show somewhere if you had good enough eyes, but now I knew better. However, I was using my eyes. The one nearest me was a lanky middle-aged guy named Ormond Leddegard. He may have been expert at handling labor-management relations, which was how he made a living, but he was a fumbler with his fingers. Getting out a pack of cigarettes, and matches, and lighting up, he was all thumbs, and that would have put him low on the list if it hadn't been for the possibility that he was being subtle. If I could figure that thumbs wouldn't have been up to the job of sneaking a pillbox from a cluttered table, making a substitution, and returning the box without detection, so could he. Of course that little point could be easily settled by having a good man, say Saul Panzer, spend a couple of days interviewing a dozen or so of his friends and acquaintances.

Next to him, with her legs crossed just right to be photographed from any angle, was Fifi Goheen. The leg-crossing technique was automatic, from an old habit. Seven or eight years ago she had been the Deb of the Year and no magazine would have dared to go to press without a shot of her; then it became all a memory; and now she was a front-page item as a murder suspect. She hadn't married. It was said that a hundred males, lured by the attractions, opening their mouths for the big proposition, had seen the hard glint in her lovely dark eyes and lost their tongues. So she was still Miss Fifi Goheen, living with Pop and Mom on Park Avenue.

Beyond her in the arc facing Wolfe's desk was Benjamin Rackell, whose check had been deposited in our bank that afternoon, with his long narrow face more mournful even than the day before. At his right was a specimen who was a female anatomically but otherwise a what-is-it. Her name was Della Devlin, and her age was beside the point. She was a resident buyer of novelties for out-of-town stores. There are ten thousand of her in midtown New York any weekday, and they're all being imposed on. You see it in their faces. The problem is to find out who it is that's imposing on them, and some day I may tackle it. Aside from that there was nothing visibly wrong with Della Devlin, except her ears were too big.

Next to her was a celebrity—though of course they were all celebrities for the time being, you might say ex officio. Henry Jameson Heath, now crowding fifty, had inherited money in his youth, quite a pile, but very few people in his financial bracket were speaking to him. There was no telling whether he had contributed dough to the Communist party or cause, or if so how much, but there was no secret about his being one of the chief providers and collecters of bail for the Commies who had been indicted. He had recently been indicted too, for contempt of Congress, and was probably headed for a modest stretch. He wore an old seersucker suit that was too small for him, had a round pudgy face, and couldn't look at you without staring.

Beyond Heath, at the end of the arc, was Carol Berk, the only one toward whom I had a personal attitude worth mentioning. Whenever we have a flock of guests I handle the seating, and if there is one who seems worthy of study I put her in the chair nearest mine. I had done so with this Carol Berk, but while I was in the hall admitting Leddegard, who had come last, she had switched on me, and I resented it. I felt that she deserved attention. Checking on her, along with the others, that afternoon with Lon Cohen of the *Gazette*, I had learned that she was supposed to be free-lancing as a TV contact specialist but no one actually claimed her, that she had a reputation as an extremely fast mover, and that there were six different versions of why she had left Hollywood three years ago. Added to that was the question whether it was a pleasure to look at her or not. In cases where it's a quick no, the big majority, or a quick yes, the small minority, that settles it and what the hell; but the borderline numbers take application and sound judgment. I had listed Carol Berk as one when, crossing the doorsill, she had darted a sidewise glance at me with brown eyes that were dead dull from the front. Now, in the chair she had changed to, she was a good five paces away.

Mrs. Benjamin Rackell, her lips tighter than ever, was in the red leather chair at the end of Wolfe's desk.

Wolfe's gaze swept the arc. "I won't thank you for coming," he rumbled at them, "because it would be impertinent. You are here at the request of Mr. and Mrs. Rackell. Whether you came to oblige them or because you thought it unwise not to is immaterial."

Also, it seemed to me, it was close to immaterial whether they were there or not. Apparently, since he had sent me to Foley Square and Homicide to clear, Wolfe was proceeding on the Rackell theory that Arthur had got it because a Commie or Commies had discovered that he was an FBI plant. But that theory had not been published, and Wolfe couldn't blurt it out. You don't disclose the identity of FBI undercover men, even dead ones, if you make your living as a private detective and want to keep your license. And if by any chance Arthur had fed his aunt one with a worm in it, if he had actually had no more connection with the FBI than me with the DAR—no, that was one to steer clear of.

So not only could Wolfe not come to the point, he couldn't even let out a hint of what the point was. How could he talk at all?

He talked. "I don't know," he said, "whether the police have made it clear to you how you stand. They don't like it that I'm taking a hand in this. The entrance to my house has been under surveillance since this morning, when they learned that Mr. and Mrs. Rackell had consulted me. One or more of you were probably followed here this evening. But Mr. Rackell may properly hire me, I may properly work for him, and you may properly give me information if you feel like it."

"We don't know whether we do or not." Leddegard shifted in his chair, stretching his lanky legs. "At least I don't. I came as a courtesy to people in bereavement."

"It is appreciated," Wolfe assured him. "Now for how you stand. I talked with Mr. and Mrs. Rackell yesterday, and with Mrs. Rackell again this afternoon. It is characteristic of the newspapers to focus attention on you five people; it's obvious and dramatic, and, after all, you were there when Arthur Rackell swallowed poison and died. But beyond the obvious, why you? Have the police been candid?"

"That's a damn silly question," Heath declared. He had a flat but aggressive baritone. "The police are never candid."

"I knew a candid cop once," Fifi Goheen said helpfully.

"It seems to me," Carol Berk told Wolfe, "that you're being dramatic too, getting us down here. It would have taken a slight-of-hand artist to get the pillbox from his pocket and switch a capsule and put it back, without being seen. And while the box was on the table it was right under our eyes."

Wolfe grunted. "You were all staring at it? For twelve minutes straight?"

"She didn't say we were staring at it," Leddegard blurted offensively.

"Pfui." Wolfe was disgusted. "A lummox could have managed it. Reaching for something—a roll, a cocktail glass—dropping the hand onto the box, checking glances while withdrawing the hand, changing capsules beneath the table, returning the box with another casual unnoticeable gesture. I would undertake it myself with thin inducement, and I'm not Houdini."

"Tell me something," Leddegard demanded. "I may be thick, but why did it have to be done at the restaurant? Why not before?"

Wolfe nodded. "That's not excluded, certainly. You five people were not the only ones intimate enough with Arthur Rackell to know about his pink vitamin capsules and that he took three a day, one before each meal. Nor did you have a monopoly of opportunity. However—" His glance went left. "Mrs. Rackell, will you repeat what you told me this afternoon? About Saturday evening?"

She had been keeping her eyes at Wolfe but now moved her head to take the others in. Judging from her expression as she went down the line, apparently she was convinced not that one of them was a Commie and a murderer, but that they all were—excluding her husband, of course.

She returned to Wolfe. "My husband and Arthur had spent the afternoon getting an important shipment released, and got home a little before six. They went to their rooms to take a shower and change. While Arthur was in the shower my cook and housekeeper, Mrs. Kremp, went to his room to get things out for him, shirt and socks and underwear—she's like that; she's been doing it for years. The articles he had taken from his pockets were on the bureau, and she looked in the pillbox and saw it was empty, and she got three capsules from the bottle in a drawer—it held a hundred and was half full—and put them in the box. She did that too, every day. She is a competent woman, but she's extremely sentimental."

"And she had no reason," Wolfe inquired, "for wishing your nephew dead?"

"Certainly not!"

"She has of course told the police?"

"Of course."

"Was there anyone in the apartment other than you four —you, your husband, your nephew, and Mrs. Kremp?"

"No. No one. The maid was away. My husband and I were going to the country for the weekend."

"After Mrs. Kremp put the capsules in the box, and before your nephew came from the shower to dress—did you enter your nephew's room during that period?"

"No. I didn't enter it at all."

"Did you, Mr. Rackell?"

"I did not." He sounded as mournful as he looked.

Wolfe's eyes went left to right, from Carol Berk at one end to Leddegard at the other. "Then we have Arthur Rackell bathed and dressed, the pillbox in his pocket. The police are not confiding in me, but I read newspapers. Leaving the apartment, he went down in the elevator and out to the sidewalk, and the doorman got a taxi for him. He was alone in the taxi, and it took him straight to the restaurant. The capsules left in the bottle have been examined and had not been tampered with. There we are. Are you prepared to impeach Mrs. Kremp, or Mr. or Mrs. Rackell? Can you support the assumption that one of them murdered Arthur Rackell?"

"It's not inconceivable," Della Devlin murmured.

"No," Wolfe conceded. "Nor is it inconceivable that he chose that moment and method to kill himself, nor even that a capsule of poison got into the bottle by accident. But

I exclude them as too improbable for consideration, and so will everyone else, including the police. The inquiring mind is rarely blessed with a certainty; it must make shift with assumptions; and I am assuming, on the evidence, that when Arthur arrived at the restaurant the capsules in the box in his pocket were innocent. I invite you to challenge it. If you can't the substitution was made at the restaurant, and you see how you stand. The police are after you, and so am I. One of you? Or all of you? I intend to find out."

"You're scaring me stiff," Fifi Goheen said. "I'm frail and I may collapse." She stood up. "Come on, Leddy, I'll buy you a drink."

Leddegard reached for her elbow and gave it a little shake. "Hold it, Fee," he told her gruffly. "This guy has been known to do flips. Let's see. Sit down."

"Blah. You are scared. You've got a reputation." She jerked her arm loose and took two quick steps to the edge of Wolfe's desk. Her voice rose a little. "I don't like the atmosphere here. You're too fat to look at. Orchids, for God's sake!" Her hand darted to the bowl of Miltonias, and with a flip of the wrist she sent it skidding along the slick surface and off to the floor.

There was some commotion. Mrs. Rackell jerked her feet back, away from the tumbling bowl. Carol Berk said something. Leddegard left his chair and started for Fifi, but she whirled away to Henry Jameson Heath, pressed her palms to his cheeks, and bent to him. She implored him, "Hank, I love you! Do you love me? Take me somewhere and buy me a drink."

Della Devlin sprang up, hauled off, and smacked Fifi on the side of the head. It was not merely a tap, and Fifi, off balance, nearly toppled. Heath came upright and was between them. Della stood, glaring and panting. They held the tableau long enough for a take, then Fifi broke it up by addressing Della past Heath's shoulder.

"That won't help any, Del. Can he help it when he's with you if he wishes it was me? Can I help it? This only makes it worse. If he'll buy a new suit and quit bailing out Commies and stay out of jail, I may make him happy." She touched Heath's cheek with her fingertips. "Say when,

Hank." She swerved around him to the desk and told Wolfe, "Look, you buy me a drink."

I was there, retrieving the bowl. The water wouldn't hurt the rug. Taking her arm firmly, I escorted her across to the table by the big globe, which Fritz and I had outfitted, and told her to name it. She said Scotch on the rocks, and I made it ample. The others, invited, stated their preferences, and Carol Berk came to help me. Rackell, who had been between Della and Fifi, decided to move and went to Carol's chair, so when we had finished serving she took his.

Throughout the interlude two had neither moved nor spoken—Mrs. Rackell and Wolfe. Now Wolfe sent his eyes from left to right and back again.

"I trust," he said sourly, "that Miss Goheen has completed her impromptu performance. I was trying to make it clear that you five people are in a fix. I'm not going to pester you about your positions and movements at the restaurant that evening, what you saw or didn't see; if there was anything in that to point or eliminate the police would have already acted on it and I'm too far behind. I might spend a few hours digging at you, trying to find a reason why one or more of you wanted Arthur Rackell dead, but the police have had four days on that too, and I doubt if I could catch up. Since you were good enough to come here at Mrs. Rackell's request, I suppose you would be willing to answer some questions, but there doesn't seem to be any worth asking. Have you people been together at any time since Saturday evening?"

Glances were exchanged. Leddegard inquired, "Do you mean all five of us?"

"Yes."

"No, we haven't."

"Then I should think you would want to talk. Go ahead. I'll drink some beer and eavesdrop. Of course at least one of you will be on guard, but the others can speak freely. You might say something useful."

Carol Berk, now nearer me, let out a little snort. Fritz had brought a tray, and Wolfe opened a bottle, poured, waited for the foam to reach the right level, and drank. Nobody said a word.

Leddegard spoke. "It doesn't seem to work. Did you expect it to?"

"We ought to make it work," Fifi declared. "I think he's damn considerate even if he is fat, and we should help." Her head turned. "Carol, let's talk."

"Glad to," Carol agreed. "You start. Shoot."

"Well, how's this? We all knew Arthur was practically a commissar, I always called him comrade, and we knew his aunt and uncle hated it, and he was afraid he might lose his job and have to go on relief but he was so damn brave and honest he couldn't keep his mouth shut. We all knew that?"

"Of course."

"Did you know this too? He told me—a week ago today, I think it was. His aunt put it to him, reform or out on the street, and he told her he was secretly working for the FBI, spying on the Commies, but he wasn't. He thought the FBI was practically the Gestapo. I told him he shouldn't—"

"That's a lie!"

Mrs. Rackell didn't shout but she put lots of feeling in it. All eyes went to her. Her husband got up and put a hand on her shoulder. There were murmurs.

"That's an infamous lie," she said. "My nephew was a patriotic American. More than you are, all of you. All of you!" She left her chair. "I've had enough of this. I shouldn't have come. Come, Ben, we're going."

She marched out. Rackell muttered to Wolfe, "A shock for her—a real shock—I'll phone you—" and trotted after her. I went to the hall to let them out, but she had already opened the door and was on the stoop, and Rackell followed. I shut the door and went back to the office.

They were buzzing. Fifi had started them talking, all right. Wolfe was refilling his glass, watching the foam rise. I crossed to Fifi and took her glass and went to the table to replenish it, thinking she had earned a little service. She was the center of the buzzing, supplying the details of her revelation. She was sure Arthur had not been stringing her; he had told her in strict confidence, at a place and time she declined to specify, that he had told his aunt a barefaced lie—that he was working for the FBI and it must not be known. No, she hadn't told the police. She didn't like the police, especially a Lieutenant Rowcliff, who had questioned her three times and was a lout.

I looked and listened and tried to decide if Fifi was putting on an act. She was hard to tag. Was one of the others covering, and if so which one? I reached no conclusion and had no hunch. They were all interested and inquisitive, even Della Devlin, though she didn't address Fifi directly.

The only one who knew I was there was Carol Berk, who sent me a slanting glance and saw me catch it. I raised a brow at her. "What is it, a pitchout?"

"You name it." She smiled, the way she might smile at a panhandler, humane but superior. "Why, who's on base?"

I decided it right then, she was worth looking at, if for nothing else, to find out what she was keeping back. "They're loaded," I told her. "Five of you. It's against the rules. The umpire won't allow it. Mr. Wolfe is the umpire."

"He looks to me more like the backstop," she said indifferently.

I saw that it might be necessary, if events permitted, to find an opportunity to spend enough time with her to make it clear that I didn't like her.

All of a sudden Fifi Goheen let fly again. Returning from the bar with her second refill, she brought the bottle of Scotch along and poured a good three fingers in Wolfe's beer glass. She put the bottle on his desk, leaned over to stretch an arm and pat him on top of the head, straightened up, and grinned at him.

"Get high," she said urgently.

He glared at her.

"Do a flip," she commanded.

He glared.

"It's a damn shame," she declared. "The cops aren't speaking to you, and here you're buying the drinks and we're not even sociable. Why shouldn't we tell you what the cops have already found out? If they're any good they have. Take Miss Devlin here." She waved a hand. "Dozens of people will tell you that she would have got Hank Heath

to make it legal long ago if Arthur hadn't told him something about her, God knows what. Any woman would kill
a man for that. And—"

"Shut up, Fee!" Leddegard barked at her.

"Let her rave," Della Devlin said, white-faced.

Fifi ignored them. "And Mr. Leddegard, who is a dear
friend of mine, with him it's a question of his wife—don't
be a fool, Leddy. Everybody knows it." Back to Wolfe.
"She went to South America with Arthur a couple of years
ago and caught a disease and died there. I have no idea why
Mr. Leddegard waited so long to kill him."

She drained her glass and put it on the desk. "This Arthur Rackell," she said, "was quite a guy, of his kind. Carol
Berk and I discovered only a month ago that he was driving
double, by a little mischance I'd rather not describe. It was
quite embarrassing. I don't know how she felt about it, you
can ask her, but I know about me. All I needed was the
poison, and all you need is to find out how I got it. I understand that potassium cyanide is used for a lot of things and
is easy to get if you really want it. Then there's Hank
Heath. He thought Arthur had me taped, which was true
in a way, but would a man kill another man just to get a
woman, even one as pure and beautiful as me? You can
ask him. No, I'll ask him."

She wheeled. "Would you, Hank?" She wheeled again
to Wolfe. "As you see, that was quite a dinner party Arthur
got up, but he doesn't deserve all the credit. I dared him to.
I wanted a good audience, one that would appreciate—hey,
that hurts!"

Heath was beside her, gripping her arm. She jerked away
and bumped into Della Devlin, also out of her chair. Carol
Berk said something, and so did Leddegard. Heath spoke to
Wolfe. "This is a joke, and it's not funny."

Wolfe's brows went up. "It's not my joke, sir."

"You asked us to come here." His voice was soft but very
sour, and his glassy eyes looked about ready to pop out of
his round pudgy face. "Miss Goheen has been making a
fool of you, and there—"

"I have not!" Fifi was back, at his elbow. "I wouldn't
dream of it," she told Wolfe. "You know, there's some-

thing about you, fat as you are." She reached to pick up
the glass of beer and Scotch. "Open your mouth and I'll—
hey! Where you going?"

She got no reply. Out of his chair and headed for the
door, Wolfe kept on, turning left in the hall, toward the
kitchen.

That ended the party. They made remarks, especially
Leddegard and Heath, and I was sympathetic as I wrangled
them into the hall and on to the front. I went out and
stood on the stoop as they descended to the sidewalk and
headed for Tenth Avenue, just to see, but by the time they
had gone fifty paces no furtive figures had sneaked out of
areaways along the line, so I thought what the hell and
went back in. A glance in the office showed me it was
empty, and I went on to the kitchen.

Fritz was pouring something thick into a big stone jar.
Wolfe stood watching him, a slice of sturgeon in one hand
and a glass of beer in the other. His mouth was occupied.

I attacked head on. "I admit," I said, "that she was set to
toss it at you, but I was there to help wipe it off. What
good does it do to duck? There are at least eighty-six things
you have to know before you can even start, and you had
them there and didn't even try. My vacation starts next
Monday. And what about your rule on not eating at bedtime?"

He swallowed. He drank beer, put the glass and the sturgeon on the table, reached to a shelf for a Bursatto melon,
got a knife from the rack, cut the melon open, and began
spooning the seeds onto a plate.

"The precise moment," he said. "Do you want some?"

"Certainly not," I said coldly. The peach-colored meat
was so juicy there was a little pool in each half, and a breeze
from the open window carried the smell to me. I reached
for one of the halves, got a spoon, scooped out a bite—and
another . . .

Wolfe never talks business during meals, but this was
not a meal. In the middle of his melon he remarked, "For
us the past is impossible."

I darted my tongue to catch a drop of juice. "Oh. It is?"

"Yes. It would take an army. The police and the FBI

have already had four days for it. The source of the poison. Mrs. Kremp. Mrs. Rackell's surmise of the motive. Mr. Heath is presumbably a Communist, but what about the others? Anyone might be a Communist, just as anyone might have a hidden carcinoma."

He scooped a bite of melon and dealt with it. "What of the motives suggested by that fantastic female buffoon? Are any of them authentic, and if so which one or ones? That alone would need a regiment. As for the police and the FBI, we have nothing to bargain with. Are they all Communists? Were they all in on it? Must we expose not one murderer but five? All those questions and others would have to be answered. How long would it take?"

"A year ought to do it."

"I doubt it. The past is hopeless. There's too much of it."

I raised my shoulders and let them drop. "Okay, you don't have to rub it in. So we cross it off. Do I draw a check to Rackell for his three grand tonight or wait till morning?"

"Have I asked you to draw a check?"

"No, sir."

He picked up the slice of sturgeon and took a bite. He never skimped on his chewing, and it took him a good four minutes to finish. Meanwhile I disposed of my melon.

"Archie," he said.

"Yes, sir."

"How does Mr. Heath feel about Miss Goheen?"

"Well." I considered. "There are different ways of putting it. I would say something like you would feel about a dish of stewed terrapin with sherry—within your sight and smell—if you thought you knew how it would taste but had never had any."

He grunted. "Don't be fanciful. It's a serious question in a field where you are qualified as an expert and I'm not. Is his appetite deeply aroused? Would he take a risk for her?"

"I don't know how he is on risks, but I saw how he looked at her and how he reacted when she touched him. Also I saw Della Devlin, and so did you. I would say he would try crossing a high shaky bridge with a wind blowing, but not unless it had rails."

"That was the impression I got. We'll have to try it."

"Try what?"

"A shove. A dig in their ribs. If their past is too much for us, their future isn't, or shouldn't be. We'll have to try it. If it doesn't work we'll try again." He was scowling. "The best I can give it is one chance in twenty. Confound it, it requires the cooperation of Mrs. Rackell, so I'll have to see her again; that can't be helped."

He scooped a bite of melon. "You'll need some instructions. I'll finish this, and we'll go to the office."

He put the bite where it belonged and concentrated on his taste buds.

IV

IT DIDN'T work out as scheduled. The program called for getting Mrs. Rackell to the office at eleven o'clock the next morning, Thursday, but when I phoned a little before nine the maid said it was too early to disturb her. At ten she hadn't called back, and I tried again and got her. I explained that Wolfe had an important confidential question to put to her, and she said she would be at the office not later than eleven-thirty. Shortly before eleven she phoned again to say that she had called her husband at his office, and it had been decided if the question was important and confidential they should both be present to consider it. Her husband would be free for an hour or so after lunch but had a four-o'clock appointment he would have to keep. We finally settled for six o'clock, and I called Rackell at his office and confirmed it.

Henry Jameson Heath was on the front page of the *Gazette* again that morning, not in connection with homicide. Once more he had refused to disclose the names of contributors to the fund for bail for the indicted Communists and apparently he was going to stick to it no matter how much contempt he rolled up. The day's installment on the Rackell murder was on page seven, and there wasn't enough meat in it to feed a cricket. As for me, after an hour at the phone, locating Saul Panzer and Fred Durkin and Orrie Cather and passing them the word, I might as well have gone to the ball game. Wolfe had given me plenty of instructions, but I couldn't act on them until and unless the clients agreed to string along.

Mrs. Rackell arrived first, at six on the dot. A minute later Wolfe came down from the plant rooms, and she started in on him. She had the idea that he was responsible for Fifi Goheen's slanderous lie about her dead nephew, since it had been uttered in his office, and what did he propose to do about it? Why didn't he have her arrested? Wolfe controlled himself fairly well, but his tone was beginning to get sharp when the doorbell rang and I beat it to the front to let Rackell in. He jogged past me to the office on his short legs, nodded at Wolfe, kissed his wife on the cheek, dropped onto a chair, wiped his long narrow face with a handkerchief, and asked wearily, "What is it? Did you get anywhere with them?"

"No." Wolfe was short. "Not to any conclusion."

"What's this important question?"

"It's blunt and simple. I need to know whether you want the truth enough to pay for it, and if so how much."

Rackell looked at his wife. "What's he talking about?"

"We haven't discussed it," Wolfe told him. "We've been considering a point your wife raised, which I regard as frivolous. This question of mine—perhaps I should call it a suggestion. I have one to offer."

"What?"

"First I'll give you the basis for it." Wolfe leaned back and half closed his eyes. "You heard me tell those five people yesterday why it is assumed that one of them substituted the capsules. On that assumption, after further talk with them, I stack another: that it is highly improbable that the substitution could have been made, under the circumstances as established, entirely unobserved. It would have required a coincidence of remarkable dexterity and uncommon luck, and I will not accept such a coincidence except on weighty evidence. So, assuming that the substitution was made in the restaurant, I also assume, for a test at least, that one of the others saw it and knows who did it. In short, that there was an eyewitness to the murder."

Rackell's mournful face did not light up with interest. His lips were puckered, making the droop at the corners more pronounced. "That may be," he conceded, "but what good does it do if he won't talk?"

"I propose to make him talk. Or her."

"How?"

Wolfe rubbed his chin with a thumb and forefinger. His eyes moved to Mrs. Rackell and back to the husband. "This sort of thing," he said, "requires delicacy, discretion, and reticence. I'll put it this way. I will not conspire to get a man punished for a crime he did not commit. It is true that all five of those people may be Communists and therefore enemies of this country, but that does not justify framing one of them for murder. My purpose is clear and innocent—to expose the real murderer and bring him to account; and I suggest a devious method only because no other seems likely to succeed. Evidently the police, after five days on it, are up a tree, and so is the FBI—if it is engaged, and you think it is. I want to earn my fee, and I wouldn't mind the kudos."

Rackell was frowning. "I still don't know exactly what you're suggesting."

"I know it; I've been long-winded. I didn't want you to misunderstand." Wolfe came forward in his chair and put his palms on the desk. "The eyewitness is obviously reluctant. I suggest that you consent to provide twenty thousand dollars, to be paid only if my method succeeds. That will cover my fee for the unusual service I will render and also any extraordinary expense I may incur. Two things must be understood: you approve the expenditure in your interest, and the express purpose is to catch the guilty person." He upturned his palms. "There it is."

"My God. Twenty thousand." Rackell shook his head. "That's a lot of money. You mean you want a check for that amount now?"

"No. To be paid if and when earned. An oral commitment will do. Mr. Goodwin hears us and has a good memory."

Rackell opened his mouth and closed it again. He looked at his wife. He looked back at Wolfe. "Look here," he said earnestly, "maybe I'm thickheaded. It sounds to me as if what this amounts to is bribing a witness. With my money."

"Don't be a fool, Ben," his wife said sharply.

"I think you misunderstand," Wolfe told him. "To bribe is to influence corruptly by some consideration. Anyone who receives any of your money through me will get it only as an inducement to tell the truth. Influence, yes. Corrupt, surely not. As for the amount, I don't wonder that you hesitate. It's quite a sum, but I wouldn't undertake it for less."

Rackell looked at his wife again. "What did you mean, Pauline, don't be a fool?"

"I meant you'd be a fool not to do it, of course." She felt so strongly about it that her lips moved. "It was you who wanted to come to Mr. Wolfe in the first place, and now when he really wants to do something you talk about bribing. If it's the money, I have plenty of my own and I'll pay—" She stopped abruptly, tightening her lips. "I'll pay half," she said. "That's fair enough; we'll each pay half." She went to Wolfe. "Who is it, that Goheen woman?"

Wolfe ignored her. He asked Rackell, "Well, sir? How about it?"

Rackell didn't like it. He avoided his wife's gaze, but he knew it was on him, and it was pressing. He even looked at me, as if my eye might somehow help, but I was deadpan. Then he returned to Wolfe.

"All right," he said.

"You accept the proposal as I made it?"

"Yes. Only I'll pay it. I'd rather not—I'd rather pay it myself. You said to be paid if and when earned. Who decides whether you've earned it or not?"

"You do. I doubt if that will be a bone to pick."

"A question my wife asked—do you know who the eyewitness is?"

"Your wife was witless to ask it. If I knew would I tell you? Or would you want me to? Now?"

Rackell shook his head. "No, I guess not. No, I can see that it's better just to let you—" He left it hanging. "Is there anything else you want to say about it?"

Wolfe said there wasn't. Rackell got up and stood there as if he would like to say something but didn't know what. I arose and moved toward the door. I didn't want to be rude to a client who had just bought a suggestion that would cost him twenty grand, but now that he had okayed it I had a job to do and I wanted to get going. I still didn't know where Wolfe thought he was headed for, but the sooner I got started on my instructions the sooner I would know. They finally came, and I went ahead and opened the front door for them. She held his elbow going down the stoop. I shut the door and rejoined Wolfe in the office.

"Well?" I demanded. "Do I proceed?"

"Yes."

"It's nearly half-past six. If I offer to buy her a meal—I doubt if that's the right approach."

"You know the approaches to women, I don't."

"Yeah." I sat at my desk and pulled the phone to me. "If you ask me this stunt you've hatched is a swell approach to a trip to the hoosegow. For both of us."

He grunted. I started dialing a number.

V

NEW YORK can have pleasant summer evenings when it wants to, and that was one of them—warm but not hot and not muggy. I paid the taxi driver when he rolled to the curb at the address on Fifty-first Street east of Lexington, got out, and took a look. In bright sunshine the old gray brick building would probably show signs of wear and tear, but now in twilight it wasn't too bad. Entering the vestibule, I scanned the tier of names on the wall panel. The one next to the top said DEVLIN–BERK. I pushed the button, shoved the door open when the click came, went in, glanced around for an elevator and saw none, and started to climb stairs. Three flights up a door stood open, and there waiting was Della Devlin.

I told her hello, friendly but not profuse. She nodded, not so friendly, hugged the wall to let me pass, shut the door, and went by me to lead the way through an arch into a living room. I sent my eyes around with an expression of comradely interest. The chairs and couch were attractive and cool in summer slips. There were shelves of books. The windows were on the street, and there were three doors besides the arch, two of them standing open and one not quite closed.

She sat and invited me to. "I can't imagine," she said in a louder voice than seemed necessary, in spite of the street noises from the open windows, "what you want to ask me that's so mysterious."

Sitting, I regarded her. Only one corner lamp was on, and in the dim light she wasn't at all bad looking. With smaller ears she would have been a worthy specimen, with no glare on her.

"It's not mysterious," I protested. "As I said on the phone, it's private and confidential, that's all. Mr. Wolfe felt it would be an imposition to ask you to come to his office again, so he sent me. Miss Berk is out, is she?"

"Yes, she went to a show with a friend. *Guys and Dolls.*"

"Fine. It's a good show. This really is confidential, Miss Devlin. So we're alone?"

"Certainly we are. What is it, anyhow?"

There were three things wrong. First, I had a hunch, and my batting average on hunches is high. Second, she was talking too loud. Third, her telling me where Carol Berk was, even naming the show, was off key.

"The reason it's so confidential," I said, "is simply that you ought to decide for yourself what you want to do. I doubt if you realize what lengths other people may go to help you decide. You say we're alone, but it wouldn't surprise me a bit—"

I sprang up, marched across to the door that wasn't quite closed, thinking it the most likely, and jerked it open. Behind me a little smothered shriek came from Della Devlin. In front of me, backed up against closet shelves piled with cartons and miscellany, was Carol Berk. One look at her satisfied me on one point—what her eyes were like when something happened that really aroused her.

I stepped back. Della Devlin was at my elbow, jabbering. I gripped her arm hard enough to hurt a little and addressed Carol Berk as she emerged from the closet. "My God, do I look like that big a sap? Maybe your sidewise glance isn't as keen as you think—"

Della was yapping at me. "You get out! Get out!"

Carol stopped her. "Let him stay, Della." She was calm and contemptuous. "He's only a crummy little stooge, trying to slip one over for his boss. I'll be back in an hour or so."

She moved. Della, protesting, caught her arm, but she pulled loose and left through one of the open doors. There were sounds in the adjoining room, then she appeared again with a thing on her head and a jacket and handbag, and passed through to the foyer. The outer door opened and then closed. I crossed to a window and stuck my head out and in a minute saw her emerge to the sidewalk and turn west.

I went back to my chair and sat. The open closet door was unsightly, and I got up and closed it and then sat again. "Just forget it," I said cheerfully. "The closet was a bum idea anyhow; she would have stifled in there. Sit down and relax while I try and slip one over for my boss."

She stood. "I'm not interested in anything you have to say."

"Then you shouldn't have let me in. Certainly you shouldn't have stuck Miss Berk in that closet. Let's get it over with. I merely want to find out whether you have any use for ten thousand dollars."

She gawked. "Whether I what?"

"Sit down and I'll tell you."

She went to a chair and sat, and I shifted position to be more comfortable facing her. "First I want to tell you a couple of things about murder investigations. In—"

"I've heard all I want to about murder."

"I know you have, but that's one of the things. When you get involved in one it's not a question of what or how much you want to hear. That's the one question nobody asks you. Until and unless the Rackell case is solved, with the answers all in, you'll be hearing about it the rest of your life. Face it, Miss Devlin."

She didn't say anything. She clasped her hands.

"The other thing about murder investigations. Someone gets murdered, and the cops go to work on it. Everybody that might possibly have a piece of useful information gets questioned. Say they question fifty different people. How many of the fifty answer every question truthfully? Maybe ten, maybe only four or five. Ask any experienced homicide man. They know it and they expect it, and that's why, when they think it's worth it, they go over the same questions with the same person again and again, after the truth. They often get it that way and they nearly always do with people who have cooked up a story, something they did or saw, with details. Of course you're not one of those. You haven't cooked up a detailed story. You have only answered a simple question 'No' instead of 'Yes.' They can't catch you—"

"What question? What do you mean?"

"I'm coming to it. I want—"

"Do you mean I lied? About what?"

I shook my head, not to call her a liar. "Wait till I get to it. You would of course show shocked surprise if I made the flat statement that Fifi Goheen murdered Arthur Rackell by changing his capsules at the restaurant that evening and that you saw her do it. Naturally you would, since the police have asked you if you saw anyone perform that action or any part of it, and you have answered no. Wouldn't you?"

She was frowning, concentrated. Her hands were still clasped. "But you—you haven't made any such statement."

"Right. I'd rather put it another way. Nero Wolfe has

his own way of investigating and his own way of reaching conclusions. He has concluded that if he sends me to see you, to ask you to tell the police that you saw Fifi Goheen substituting the capsules, it will serve the interest of truth and justice. So he sent me, and I'm asking you. It will be embarrassing for you, but not so bad. As I explained, it won't be the first time they've had somebody suddenly remembering something. You can say you and Miss Goheen have been friends and you hated to come out with it, but now you see you have to. You can even say I came here and persuaded you to speak, if you want to, but you certainly shouldn't mention the ten thousand dollars. That—"

"What ten thousand dollars?"

"I'm telling you. Mr. Wolfe has also concluded that it would not be reasonable to expect you to undergo such embarrassment without some consideration. He has made a suggestion to Mr. and Mrs. Rackell, and they have agreed to provide a certain sum of money. Ten thousand of it will come to you, in appreciation of your cooperation in the cause of justice. It will be given you in cash, in currency, within forty-eight hours after you have done your part—and we'll have to discuss that, exactly what you'll tell the police. Speaking for Nero Wolfe, I guarantee the payment within forty-eight hours, or, if you want to, come down to his office with me now and he'll guarantee it himself. Don't ask me what it was that made him conclude that Fifi Goheen did it and that you saw her, because I don't know. Anyhow, if he's right, and he usually is, she'll only be getting what she deserves. You know that's true."

I stopped. She sat motionless, staring at me. There wasn't much light, and I couldn't tell anything from her eyes, but they looked absolutely blank. As the seconds grew to a minute and on I began to think I had literally stupefied her, and I gave her a nudge.

"Have I made it plain?"

"Yes," she mumbled, "you've made it plain."

Suddenly a shudder ran over her whole body, her head dropped forward, and her hands lifted to cover her face, her elbows on her knees. The shudder quit, and she froze like that. She held it so long that I decided another nudge

was required, but before I got it out she straightened up
and demanded, "What made you think I would do such a
thing?"

"I don't think. Mr. Wolfe does the thinking. I'm just a
crummy little stooge."

"You'd better go. Please go!"

I stood up and I hesitated. My feeling was that I had
run through it smooth as silk, as instructed, but at that
point I wasn't sure. Should I make a play of trying to
crowd her into a yes or no, or leave it hanging? I couldn't
stand there forever, debating it with her staring at me, so
I told her, "I do think it's a good offer. The number's in
the phone book."

She had nothing to tell my back as I walked to the foyer.
I let myself out, decended the three flights, walked to Lexington, found a phone booth in a drugstore, and dialed the
number I knew best. In a moment Wolfe's voice was in my
ear.

"Okay," I said. "I'm in a booth. I just left her."

"In what mind?"

"I'm not sure. She had Carol Berk hid in a closet. After
that had been attended to and we were alone I followed
the script, and she was impressed. I'm so good at explaining
things that she didn't have to ask questions. The light
wasn't very good, but as far as I could tell the prospect of
collecting ten grand wasn't absolutely repulsive to her, and
neither was the idea of flipping Miss Goheen into the
soup. She was torn. She told me to go, and I though it
wise to oblige. When I left she was in a clinch with herself."

"What is she going to do?"

"Don't quote me. But I told her we'd have to discuss
exactly what she would tell the cops, so we'll hear from
her if she decides to play. Do you want my guesses?"

"Yes."

"Well. On her spilling it to the cops, the one thing that
would spoil it, forty to one against. That isn't how her
mind will work. On her deciding to play ball with us,
twenty to one against. She's not tough enough. On her
just keeping it to herself, fifteen to one against. On general

principles. On her telling Miss Goheen, ten to one against. She hates her too much. On telling Carol Berk, two to one against, but I wouldn't dig deep on that one either way. On her telling Mr. H, even money, no matter who is a Commie and who isn't. It would show him how fine and big-hearted and noble she is. She could be, at that. It has been done. Is Saul there?"

"Yes. I never spent anybody's money, not even my own, on a slimmer chance."

"Especially your own. And incidentally sticking my neck out. You don't know the meaning of fear when it comes to sticking my neck out. Do we proceed?"

"What alternative is there?"

"None. Has Saul got his men there?"

"Yes."

"Tell him to step on it and meet me at the northeast corner of Sixty-ninth and Fifth Avenue. She could be phoning Heath right now."

"Very well. Then you'll come home?"

I said I would, hung up, and got out of the oven. Nothing would have been more appreciated right then than a large coke-and-lime with the ice brushing my lips, but it was possible that Della was already phoning him and he was at home to get the call, so I marched on by the fountain and out. A taxi got me to the corner of Sixty-ninth and Fifth in six minutes. My watch said 9:42.

I strolled east on Sixty-ninth and stopped across the street from the canopied entrance of the towering tenement of which Henry Jameson Heath was a tenant. It was no casing problem for me, since Saul Panzer had been there in the afternoon to make a survey and spot foxholes. That was elaborate but desirable, because it was to be a very fancy tail, using three shifts of three men each, with Saul in charge of one, Fred Durkin of the second, and Orrie Cather of the third. Fifteen skins an hour that setup would cost, which was quite a disbursement on what Wolfe had admited was a one-in-twenty chance. Seeing no one but a uniformed doorman in evidence around the canopy, I moseyed back to the corner.

A taxi pulled up, and three men got out. Two of them

were just men whose names I knew and with whose records I was fairly familiar, but the third was Saul Panzer, the one guy I want within hearing the day I get hung on the face of a cliff with jet eagles zooming at me. With his saggy shoulders and his face all nose, he looks one-fifth as strong and hardy, and one-tenth as smart, as he really is. I shook hands with him, not having seen him for a week or so, and nodded to the other two.

"Is there anything to say?" I asked him.

"I don't think so. Mr. Wolfe filled me in."

"Okay, take it. You know the Homicide boys may be on him too?"

"Sure. We'll try not to trip on 'em."

"You know it's a long shot and the only bet we've got? So lose him quick, what do we care."

"We'll lose him or die."

"That's the spirit. That's what puts statues of private detectives in the park. See you on the witness stand."

I left them. My immediate and urgent objective was Madison Avenue for a coke-and-lime, but I went a block north to Seventieth Street. Sixty-ninth Street now belonged to Saul and his squad.

VI

A T ELEVEN o'clock the next morning, Friday, I sat in the office listening to the clank of Wolfe's elevator as it brought him down from the plant rooms.

There had been no cheep from Della Devlin, but we hadn't wanted one anyway. What we wanted we had got, at least the first installment. At 12:42 Thursday night Saul had phoned that Heath had checked in at Sixty-ninth Street, arriving in a taxi, alone. That was all for the night. At 6:20 in the morning he had phoned that Fred Durkin and his two men had taken over and had been briefed on the terrain. And at 10:23 Fred had phoned that Heath had left his tenement and taken a taxi to 719 East Fifty-first Street and entered the building. That was the gray brick house I had visited the day before. Fred said they had seen no sign of an official tail. They were deployed. I told him he was my favorite mick and still would be if he hung on, and buzzed Wolfe in the plant rooms to inform him.

Wolfe entered, got at his desk, looked over the morning mail, signed a couple of checks, dictated a letter of inquiry about sausage to a man in Wisconsin, and settled down with the crossword puzzle in the London *Times*. I carried on my routine neatly and normally, making it perfectly plain that I could be just as placid as him, no matter how tense and ticklish it got. I had just finished typing the envelope for the letter and was twirling it out of the manchine when the doorbell rang. I went to the hall to answer it, took one look through the one-way glass panel, wheeled and returned to the office, and spoke.

"I guess I'm through as a bookie. I said forty to one she wouldn't spill it. Wengert and Cramer want in. We can sneak out the back way and head for Mexico."

He finished putting in a letter, with precision, before he looked up. "Is this flummery?"

"No, sir. It's them."

"Indeed." His brows went up a trifle. "Bring them in."

I went out and to the door, turned the knob, and pulled it open. "Hello hello," I said brightly. "Mr. Wolfe was saying only a minute ago that he would like to see Mr. Cramer and Mr. Wengert, and here you are."

Bright as it was, it didn't go over so well because they stepped in with the first hello and were well along the hall by the time I finished. I shut the door and followed. Entering the office, it struck me as encouraging that Wengert and Wolfe were shaking hands, but then I remembered the District Attorney who always shook hands with the defendant before he opened up, to show there was no personal feeling. Cramer usually took the red leather chair at the end of Wolfe's desk, but this time he let Wengert have it, and I moved up one of the yellow ones for him.

"I sent you my regards the other day by Goodwin," Wengert said. "I hope he remembered."

Wolfe inclined his head. "He did. Thank you."

"I didn't know then I'd be seeing you so soon."

"Nor did I."

"No, I suppose not." Wengert crossed his legs and leaned back. "Goodwin said you had taken on a job for Mr. and Mrs. Benjamin Rackell."

"That's right." Wolfe was casual. "To investigate the death of their nephew. They said he had been working for the FBI. It would have been impolitic to wander into your line of fire, so I sent Mr. Goodwin to see you."

"Let's cut the blah. You sent him to get information you could use."

Wolfe shrugged. "Confronted with omniscience, I bow. My motives are often obscure to myself, but you know all about them. Your advantage. If that was his errand, he failed. You told him nothing."

"Right. Our files are for us, not for private operators. My coming here tells you that we've got a hand in this case, but that's not for publication. If you didn't want to get into our line of fire you certainly stumbled. But officially it's a Manhattan homicide, so I'm here to listen." He nodded at Cramer. "Go ahead, Inspector."

Cramer had been holding in with difficulty. Holding in is a chronic problem with him, and it shows in various ways, chiefly by his big red face getting redder, with the color spreading lower on his thick muscular neck. He blurted at Wolfe, "Honest to God, I'm surprised! Not at Goodwin so much, but you! Subornation of perjury. Attempting to bribe a witness to give false testimony. I've known you to take some fat risks, but holy saints, this ain't risking it, it's yelling for it!"

Wolfe was frowning. "Are you saying that Mr. Goodwin and I have suborned perjury?"

"You've tried to!"

"Good heavens, that's a serious charge. You must have warrants. Serve them, by all means."

"Just give it to him, Inspector," Wengert advised.

Cramer's head jerked to me. "Did you go last evening to the apartment of Della Devlin on Fifty-first Street?"

"It's hotter than yesterday," I stated.

"I asked you a question!"

"This is infantile," Wolfe told him. "You must know the legal procedure with suspected felons. We do."

"Just give it to him," Wengert repeated.

Cramer was glaring at Wolfe. "What you know about legal procedures. Okay. Yesterday you sent Goodwin to see Della Devlin. In your name he offered her ten thousand dollars to testify falsely that she saw Fifi Goheen take the pillbox from the table, remove a capsule and replace it with another, and put the box back on the table. He said the money would be supplied by Mr. and Mrs. Rackell and would be handed her in currency after she had so testified. I shouldn't have said subornation of perjury, I should have said attempt. Now do I ask Goodwin some questions?"

"I'd like to ask him one myself." Wolfe's eyes moved. "Archie. Is what Mr. Cramer just said true?"

"No, sir."

"Then don't answer questions. A policeman has no right to make an inaccurate statement to a citizen about his actions and then order him to answer questions about it." He went to Cramer. "We could drag this out interminably. Why not resolve it sensibly and conclusively?" He came to me. "Archie, get Miss Devlin on the phone and ask her to come down here at once."

I turned and started to dial.

"Cut it, Goodwin," Wengert snapped. I went on dialing. Cramer, who can move when he wants to, left his chair and was by me, pushing down the button. I cocked my head to look up at him. He scowled down at me. I put it back in the cradle. He returned to his chair.

"Then we'll have to change the subject," Wolfe said dryly. "Surely your position is untenable. You want to bullyrag us for what Mr. Goodwin, as my agent, said to Miss Devlin; the first thing to establish is what was actually said; and the only satisfactory way to establish it is to have them both here. Yet you not only didn't bring her with you, you are even determined that we shall not communicate with her. Obviously you don't want her to know what's going on. It's quite preposterous, but I draw no conclusion. It's hard to believe that the New York police and the FBI would conspire to bamboozle a citizen, even me."

Cramer was reddening up again.

Wengert cleared his throat. "Look, Wolfe," he said, not belligerently, "we're here to talk sense."

"Good. Why not start?"

"I am. The interest of the people and government of the United States is involved in this case. My job is to protect that interest. I know you and Goodwin can keep your mouths shut when you want to. I am now talking off the record. Is that understood?"

"Yes, sir."

"Goodwin?"

"Good here."

"See that you keep it good. Arthur Rackell told his aunt that he was working with the FBI. That was a lie. He was either a member of the Communist party or a fellow traveler, we're not sure which. We don't know who he told, besides his aunt, that he was with the FBI, but we're working on it and so are the police. He may have been killed by a Communist who heard it somehow and believed it. There were other motives, personal ones, but the Communist angle comes first until and unless it's ruled out. So you can see why we're in on it. The public interest is involved, not only of this city and state but the whole country. You see that?"

"I saw it," Wolfe muttered, "when I sent Mr. Goodwin to see you day before yesterday."

"We'll skip that." Wengert didn't want to offend. "The point is, what about you? I concede that all you're after is to catch the murderer and collect a fee. But we know you sent Goodwin to Miss Devlin yesterday to offer to pay her to say that she saw Miss Goheen in the act. We also know that you are not likely to pull such a stunt just for the hell of it. You knew exactly what you were doing and why you were doing it. You say you have regard for the public interest. All right, the inspector here represents it, and so do I, and we want you to open up for us. We confidently expect you to. What and whom are you after, and where does that stunt get you?"

Wolfe was regarding him sympathetically through half-closed eyes. "You're not a nincompoop, Mr. Wengert." The eyes moved. "Nor you, Mr. Cramer."

"That's something," Cramer growled.

"It is indeed, considering the average. But your coming here to put this to me, either peremptorily or politely, was ill considered. Shall I explain?"

"If it's not too much bother."

"I'll be as brief as possible. Let us make a complex supposition—that I got Mr. and Mrs. Rackell's permission for an extraordinary disbursement for a stated purpose; that I sent Mr. Goodwin to see Miss Devlin; that he told her I had concluded that Miss Goheen had murdered Arthur Rackell and she had seen the act; that I suggested that she should inform the police of the fact; and that, as compensation for her embarrassment and distress, I engaged to pay her a large sum of money which would be provided by Mr. and Mrs. Rackell."

Wolfe upturned a palm. "Supposing I did that, it was not an attempt to suborn perjury, since it cannot be shown that I intended her to swear falsely, but certainly I was exposing myself to a claim for damages from Miss Goheen. That was a calculated risk I had to take, and whether the calculation was sound depended on the event. There was also a risk of being charged with obstruction of justice, and that too depended on the event. Should it prove to serve justice instead of obstructing it, and should Miss Goheen suffer no unmerited damage, I would be fully justified. I hope to be. I expect to be."

"Then you can—"

"If you please. But suppose, having done all that, I now admit it to you and tell you my calculations and intentions. Then you'll either have to try to head me off or be in it with me. It would be jackassery for you to head me off—take my word for it; it would be unthinkable. But it would also be unthinkable for you to be in it, either actively or passively. Whatever the outcome may be, you cannnot afford to be associated with an offer to pay a large sum of money to a person involved in a murder case for disclosing a fact, even an authentic one. Your positions forbid it. I'm a private citizen and can stand it; you can't. What the devil did you come here for? If I'm headed for defeat, opprobrium, and punishment, then I am. Why dash up here only to get yourselves confronted with unthinkable alternatives?"

Wolfe fluttered a hand. "Luckily, this is just talk. I was merely discussing a complex supposition. To return to reality, I will be glad to give you gentlemen any information that you may properly require—and Mr. Goodwin too, of course. So?"

They looked at each other. Cramer let out a snort. Wengert pulled at his ear and gazed at me, and I returned the gaze, open-faced and perfectly innocent. He found that not helpful and transferred to Wolfe.

"You called the turn," he said, "when you told Goodwin to phone Miss Devlin. I should have forseen that. That was dumb."

The phone rang, and I swiveled and got it. "Nero Wolfe's office, Archie Goodwin speaking."

"This is Rattner."

"Oh, hello. Keep it down, my ears are sensitive."

"Durkin sent me to phone so he could stay on the subject. The subject came out of the house at seven nineteen East Fifty-first Street at eleven forty-one. He was alone. He walked to Lexington and around the corner to a drugstore and is in there now in a phone booth. I'm across the street in a restaurant. Any instructions?"

"Not a thing, thank you. Give my love to the family."

"Right."

It clicked off, and I hung up and swiveled back to rejoin the party, but apparently it was over. They were on their feet, and Wengert was turning to go. Cramer was saying, ". . . but it's not *all* off the record. I just want that understood."

He turned and followed Wengert out. I saw no point in dashing past them out to the door, since two grown

men should be up to turning a knob and pulling, but I
stepped to the hall to observe. When they were outside
and the door closed I went back in and remarked to
Wolfe, "Very neat. But what if they had let me phone
her?"

He made a face. "Pfui. If they had got it from her they
wouldn't have called on me. They would have sent for
you, possibly with a warrant. That was one of the con-
tingencies."

"They might have let me phone her anyway."

"Unlikely, since that would have disclosed their knowledge—to her and therefore to anyone—and betrayed their
informant. But if they had, while she was on her way I
would have proceeded with them, and they would have
left before she arrived."

I put the yellow chair back in place. "All the same I'm
glad they didn't and so are you. That was Rattner on the
phone, reporting for Fred. Heath was with Miss Devlin an
hour and four minutes. He left at eleven forty-one and
was in a phone booth in a drugstore when Rattner called."

"Satisfactory." He picked up his pencil and bent over
the crossword puzzle with a little sigh.

VII

JUNE twenty-first is supposed to be the longest day, but
this year it was August third. It went on for weeks after
Cramer and Wengert left. I spent it all in the office, and
it was no fun. There was only one thing that could keep
us floating, but there were a dozen that could sink us.
They might lose him. Or he might handle it by phone—
most unlikely, but not impossible. Or Wolfe might have
it figured entirely wrong; he himself gave it one in twenty.
Or Heath might meet him or her some place where they
couldn't be nailed. Or a city or federal employee might
horn in and ruin it. Or and or and or.

Five bucks an hour had been added to the outgo. If

and when the call came that would start me moving, I didn't want to waste any precious minutes or even seconds finding transportation, so Herb Aronson had his taxi parked at the filling station at the corner of Eleventh Avenue, on us. Also he came to us for lunch and again, at seven in the evening, for dinner.

Every time the phone rang and I grabbed it, I wanted it and I didn't. It might be the starting gun, but on the other hand it might be the awful news that they had lost him. Keeping a tail on a guy in New York, especially if he has an important reason for wanting privacy, needs not only great skill but also plenty of luck. We were buying the skill, in Saul and Fred and Orrie, but you can't buy luck.

The luck held, and so did they. There were two more calls from Fred, via Rattner, before two o'clock, when he was relieved by Orrie Cather. One was to report that Heath, after calls at an optician's and a bookstore, had entered a restaurant on Forty-fifth Street and was lunching with two men, not known to me as described, and the other was to tell where Orrie could find him. There was still no sign of an official tail. During the afternoon and early evening there was a series of reports from Orrie. Heath and his companions left the restaurant at 2:52, taxied to the apartment house on Sixty-ninth Street where Heath lived, and entered. At 5:35 the two men emerged and walked off. At 7:03 Heath came out and took a taxi to Chezar's restaurant, where he met Della Devlin and they dined. At 9:14 they left and taxied to the gray brick house on Fifty-first Street and went in. Heath was still in there at ten o'clock, the hour for Orrie to be relieved by Saul Panzer, and it was at the corner of Fifty-first and Lexington that Orrie and Saul connected.

By that time I would have been chewing on a railroad spike if I had had one, and Wolfe was working hard trying to be serene. Between nine-thirty and ten-thirty he made four trips to the bookshelves, trying different ones, setting a record.

I snarled at him, "What's the matter, restless?"

"Yes," he said placidly. "Are you?"

"Yes."

It came a little before eleven. The phone rang, and I got it. It was Bill Doyle.

He seemed to be panting. "I'm out of breath," he said, wasting some of it. "When he left there he got smart and started tricks. We let him spot Al and ditch him, you know how Saul works it, but even then we damn near lost him. He came to Eighty-sixth and Fifth and went in the park on foot. A woman was sitting on a bench with a collie on a leash, and he stopped and started talking to her. Saul thinks you'd better come."

"So do I. Describe the woman."

"I can't. I was keeping back and didn't get close enough."

"Where is Saul?"

"On the ground under a bush."

"Where are you?"

"Drugstore. Eighty-sixth and Madison."

"Be at the Eighty-sixth-Street park entrance. I'm coming."

I whirled and told Wolfe, "In Central Park. He met a woman with a dog. So long."

"Are you armed?"

"Certainly." I was at the door.

"They will be desperate."

"I already am."

I let myself out, ran down the stoop and to the corner. Herb was in his hack, listening to the radio. At sight of me on the lope he switched it off, and by the time I was in he had the engine started. I told him, "Eighty-sixth and Fifth," and we rolled.

We went up Eleventh Avenue instead of Tenth because with the staggered lights on Tenth you can't average better than twenty-five. On Eleventh you can make twelve or more blocks on a light if you sprint, and we sprinted. At Fifty-sixth we turned east, had fair luck crosstown, and turned left on Fifth Avenue. I told Herb to quit crawling, and he told me to get out and walk. When we reached

Eighty-sixth Street I had the door open before the wheels stopped, hopped out, and crossed the avenue to the park side.

Bill Doyle was there. He was the pale gaunt type, from reading too much about horses and believing it. I asked him, "Anything new?"

"No. I been here waiting."

"Can you show me Saul's bush without rousing the dog?"

"I can if he's still there. It's quite a ways."

"Within a hundred yards of them take to the grass. They mustn't hear our footsteps stopping. Let's go."

He entered the park by the paved path, and I trailed. The first thirty paces it was upgrade, curving right. Under a park light two young couples had stopped to have an argument, and we detoured around them. The path leveled and straightened under overhanging branches of trees. We passed another light. A man swinging a cane came striding from the opposite direction and on by. The path turned left, crossed an open space, and entered shrubbery. A little further on there was a fork, and Doyle stopped.

"They're down there a couple of hundred feet," he whispered, pointing to the left branch of the fork. "Or they were. Saul's over that way."

"Okay, I'll lead. Steer me by touch."

I stepped onto the grass and started alongside the right branch of the fork. It was uphill a little, and I had to duck under branches. I hadn't gone far when Doyle tugged at my sleeve, and when I turned he pointed to the left. "That bunch of bushes there," he whispered. "The big one in the middle. That's where he went, but I can't see him."

My sight is twenty-twenty, and my eyes had got adjusted to the night, but for a minute I couldn't pick him up. When I did the huddled hump under the bush was perfectly plain. A ripple ran up my spine. Since Saul was still there, Heath was still there too, under his eye, and almost certainly the woman with the dog was there also. Of course I couldn't see them, on account of the bushes. I considered what to do. I wanted to confront them together, before they separated, but if Saul was close enough to hear their words I didn't want to bust it up. The most attractive idea was to sneak across to Saul's bush and join him, but I might be heard, if not by them by the dog. Standing there, peering toward Saul's bush, concentrated, with Doyle beside me, I became aware of footsteps behind me, approaching along the path, but supposed it was just a late park stroller and didn't turn—until the footsteps stopped and a voice came.

"Looking for tigers?"

I wheeled. It was a flatfoot on park patrol. "Good evening, officer," I said respectfully. "Nope, just getting air."

"The air's the same if you stay on the path." He approached on the grass, looking not at us but past us, in the direction we had been gazing. Suddenly he grunted, quickened his step, and headed straight for Saul's bush. Apparently he had good eyes too. There was no time to consider. I muttered fast at Doyle's ear, "Grab his cap and run—jump, damn it!"

He did. I will always love him for it, especially for not hesitating a tenth of a second. Four leaps got him to the cop, a swoop of his hand got the cap, and away he scooted, swerving right to double back to the path. I stood in my tracks. The cop acted by reflex. Instead of ignoring the playful prank and proceeding to inspect the object under the bush, or making for me, he bounded after Doyle and his cap, calling a command to halt. Doyle, reaching the path and streaking along it, had a good lead, but the cop was no snail. They disappeared.

All that commotion changed the situation entirely. I made it double quick to the left across the grass until I reached the other fork of the path, and kept going. Around a bend, there they were—Heath seated on a bench with a woman, a big collie lying at their feet. When I stopped in front of them the collie rose to its haunches and made a noise, asking a question. I had a hand in a coat pocket.

"Tell the dog it's okay," I suggested. "I hate to shoot a dog."

"Why should you—" Heath started, and stopped. He stood up.

"Yeah, it's me," I said. "Representing Nero Wolfe. It won't help if you scream, there's two of us. Come on out, Saul. Watch the dog, it may not wait for orders."

There was a sound from the direction of the bushes, and in a moment Saul appeared, circling around to join me on the right. The dog made a noise that was more of a whine than a growl, but it didn't move. The woman put a hand on its head. I asked Saul, "Could you hear what they said?"

"Most of it. I heard enough."

"Was it interesting?"

"Yes."

"This is illegal," Heath stated. He was half choked with indignation or something. "This is an invasion—"

"Nuts. Save it; you may need it. I have a cab parked at the Eighty-sixth-Street entrance. Four of us with the dog will just fill it comfortably. Mr. Wolfe is expecting us. Let's go."

"You're armed," Heath said. "This is assault with a deadly weapon."

"I'm going home," the woman said, speaking for the first time. "I'll telephone Mr. Wolfe, or my husband will, and we'll see about this. I brought my dog to the park, and this gentleman and I happened to get into conversation. This is outrageous. You won't dare to harm my dog."

She got up, and the collie was instantly erect by her, against her knee.

"Well," I conceded, "I admit I hate to shoot a dog. I also admit that Mr. Wolfe likes himself so well that he'll steal the throne on the Day of Judgment if they don't watch him. So you go on home with Towser, and Saul and I will call on the police and the FBI, and I'll tell them what I saw, and Saul will tell them what he saw and heard. But don't make the mistake of thinking you can talk them out of believing us. We have our reputations just as you have yours."

They looked at each other. They looked at me and back at each other.

"We'll see Mr. Wolfe," the woman said.

Heath looked right and then left, as if hoping there might be someone else around to see, and then nodded at her.

"That's sensible," I told them. "You lead the way, Saul. Eighty-sixth-Street entrance."

VIII

WE LEFT the collie in Herb's taxi, parked at the curb in front of Wolfe's place. There has never been a dog in that house, and I saw no point in breaking the precedent for one who was on such strained terms with me. Herb, on advice, closed the glass panels.

I went ahead up the stoop to open the door and let them in, put them in the front room with Saul, and went through to the office.

"Okay," I told Wolfe, "it's your turn. They're here."

Behind his desk, he closed the book he had been reading and put it down. He asked, "Mrs. Rackell?"

"Yes. They were there on a bench, with dog, and Saul was behind a bush and could hear, but I don't know what. I gave them their choice of the law or you, and they preferred you. She probably thinks she can buy out. You want Saul first?"

"No. Bring them in."

"But Saul can tell you—"

"I don't need it. Or if I do—we'll see."

"You want him in too?"

"Yes."

I went and opened the connecting door and invited them, and they entered. As Mrs. Rackell crossed to the red leather chair and sat her lips were so tight there were none. Heath's face had no expression at all, but it must be hard to display feeling with that kind of round pudgy frontispiece even if you try. Saul took a chair against the far wall, but Wolfe told him to move up, and he transferred to one at the end of my desk.

Mrs. Rackell grabbed the ball. She said it was absolutely contemptible, spying on her and threatening her with the police. It was infamous and treacherous. She wouldn't tolerate it.

Wolfe let her get it out and then said dryly, "You astonish me, madam." He shook his head. "You chatter about proprieties when you are under the menace of a mortal peril. Don't you realize what I've done? Don't you know where we stand?"

"You're chattering yourself," Heath said harshly. "We were brought here under a threat. By what right?"

"I'll tell you." Wolfe leaned back. "This is no pleasure for me, so I'll hurry it—my part of it. But you need to know exactly what the situation is, for you have a vital decision to make. First let me introduce Mr. Saul Panzer." His eyes moved. "Saul, you followed Mr. Heath to a clandestine meeting with Mrs. Rackell?"

"Yes, sir."

"Then I'll risk an assumption. I assume that his purpose was to protest against her supplying funds to inculpate Miss Goheen, and to demand that the attempt be abandoned. You heard much of what they said?"

"Yes, sir."

"Did it impeach my assumption?"

"No, sir."

"Did it support it?"

"Yes, sir. Plenty."

Wolfe went to Heath. "Mr. Panzer's quality is known, though not to you until now. I think a jury will believe him, and I'm sure the police and the FBI will. My advice, sir, is to cut the loss."

"Loss?" Heath was trying to sneer but with that face he couldn't make it. "I haven't lost anything."

"You're about to. You can't help it." Wolfe wiggled a finger at him. "Must I spell it out for you? Wednesday evening, day before yesterday, when you and six others were here, I was nonplused. I had my choice of giving up or of attempting simultaneously a dozen elaborate lines of inquiry, any one of which would have strained my resources. Neither was tolerable. Since I was helpless with what had already happened, I had to try to make something happen under my eye, and I devised a stratagem—a clumsy one, but the best I could do. I made a proposal to Mr. and Mrs. Rackell. I phrased it with care, but in effect I asked for money to bribe a witness and solve the case by chicanery."

Wolfe's eyes darted to Mrs. Rackell. "And you idiotically exposed yourself."

"I did?" She was contemptuous. "How?"

"You grabbed at it. Your husband, in his innocence, was dubious, but not you. You thought that, having decided the job was beyond me, I was trying to earn a fee by knavery, and you eagerly acquiesced. Why? It was out of character and indeed preposterous. What you had said you wanted was the murderer of your nephew caught and punished, but apparently you were willing to spend a large sum of money, your own money, on a frame-up. Either that or you were excessively naive, and at least it justified speculation."

His gaze was straight at her, and she was meeting it. He went on, "So I speculated. What if you had yourself killed your nephew? As for getting the poison, that was as feasible for you as for the others. As for opportunity, you said you had not entered your nephew's room after Mrs. Kremp had been there and put the capsules in the pillbox, but could you prove it? There was nothing to my knowledge that excluded you. Your harassment of the FBI and the police could have been for assurance that you were safe. It was your husband who insisted on coming to me, and naturally you would have wanted to be present. As for motive, that would have to be explored, but for speculation there was material at hand, furnished by you. You were positive, with no real evidence for it, that your nephew had been killed by a Communist who had discovered that he was betraying the cause; you got that in first thing when you called here Tuesday with your husband. Might it not be true and you yourself the Communist?"

"Rot!" She snorted.

Wolfe shook his head. "Not necessarily. I deplore the

current tendency to accuse people of pro-communism irresponsibly and unjustly, but anybody could be one secretly, no matter what façade he presented. There was the question, if you were in fact a Communist or a sympathizer, why did you so badger your nephew that he had to pacify you by telling the lie that he was working for the FBI? Why didn't you confide in him your own devotion to the cause? Of course you didn't dare. There would have been the danger that he might recant; he might have become an ex-Communist and told all he knew, as so many have done the past year or two; and to preserve your façade for your husband and friends you had to keep after him. It must have been a severe shock when you learned, or thought you did, that he was an agent of communism's implacable enemy. It made him an imminent threat, there in your own household."

Wolfe came forward in his chair. "That was all speculation two days ago, but not now. Your meeting with Mr. Heath has made it a confident assumption. Why would you make a secret rendezvous with him? What could give him the right to demand that you withdraw the offer of money for Miss Devlin? Well. If you are secretly a Communist, almost certainly you have contributed substantial sums of money—to the party of course, but also to the bail fund; and Mr. Heath is the trustee of the bail fund and is inviting a term in jail rather than disclose the names of the contributors. So, madam, my stratagem worked—with, I confess, a full share of luck. Mr. Goodwin and I have been under some strain. Until a few minutes ago, when he entered and told me you two were here, I wouldn't have wagered a nickel on it. Now it's over, thank heaven. My assumptions are on rock. You're cooked."

"You're a conceited fool," Mrs. Rackell said flatly. For the first time I thought she was really impressive. He hadn't made a dent in her. She was still dead sure of herself. "With your crazy assumptions," she said. "I was resting on a park bench, and this Mr. Heath came along and spoke." She darted a contemptuous glance at Saul. "Whatever lies that man tells about what he heard."

Wolfe nodded. "That of course is your best position,

and no doubt you're capable of defending it against all assault, so I won't try butting it." He looked at Heath. "But yours is much weaker, and I don't see how you can hold it."

"I have withstood better men than you," Heath declared. "Men in positions of great power. Men who head the imperialist conspiracy to dominate the world."

"No doubt," Wolfe conceded. "But even if you appraise them correctly, which I question, right now you have to appraise me. I head no conspiracy to dominate anything, but I've got you in a hole you can't scramble out of. Must I spell it out for you? You're a trustee of that Communist bail fund, amounting to nearly a million dollars, and at great personal risk you are determined to keep the names of the contributors secret. Court orders haven't budged you. Obviously you prefer any alternative to disclosure of the names. But you're going to disclcose one of them to me now: Mrs. Benjamin Rackell. And the amounts and dates of her contributions. Well?"

"No comment."

"Pfui. I say you can't hold it. Consider what's going to happen. I am convinced that Mrs. Rackell murdered her nephew because she thought he was spying on Communists for the FBI, and therefore, of course, her own secret was in danger. The FBI and the police will now share that conviction. Whether it takes a day or a year, do you think there's any chance we won't get her? Knowing she had the poison, do you think we won't discover where and how she got it?"

Wolfe shook his head. "No. You'll have to ditch her. She's too hot to hold. The police will put it to you—have you any knowledge or evidence that she has been in sympathy with the Communist cause? You say no or refuse to answer. Subsequently they get such evidence, with proof that you were aware of it; it is easily possible that, through some process which you cannot avert, they will get the whole list of contributors. And instead of a brief commitment for contempt of court you'll get a considerable term for withholding vital evidence in a murder case. Besides, what of the cause you're devoted to? You know the opinion of communism held by most Americans, including me. To the odium already attached to it would you add the stigma of shielding a murderer?"

Wolfe raised his brows. "Really, Mr. Heath. There are plenty of precedents to guide you. This will be by no means the first time that an act of misguided zeal by a Communist has come home to roost. In the countries they rule the jails are full—let alone the graves—of former comrades who were indiscreet. In America, where you don't rule and I hope you never will, can you afford the luxury of shielding a murderer? No. She's too much for you. How much has she contributed and when?"

Heath's face was really something. If he hadn't inherited money he could have piled it up playing poker. From looking at him no one could have got the faintest notion how to bet.

He stood up. "I'll let you know tomorrow," he said.

Wolfe grunted. "Oh no. I want to phone the police to come for her. They'll want a statement from you. Archie?"

I got up and moved and was between the company and the door. Heath moved too. "I'm going," he said, and came. When I stood pat he swerved to circle around me. It would have been a pleasure to plug him, but I refrained and merely got his shoulder, whirled him, and propelled him a little. He stumbled but stayed upright.

"This is assault," he told Wolfe, not me. "And illegal restraint. You'll regret this."

"Bosh." Wolfe suddenly blew up. "Confound it, do you think I'm going to let you walk out to call a meeting of your Politburo? Do you think I don't know when I've got you hooked? You can't possibly hang onto her. Talk sense! Can you?"

"No," he said.

"Are you ready to disclose the facts?"

"Not to you. To the police, yes."

Mrs. Rackell snapped at him, "Have you gone mad, you fool?"

He stared at her. I've heard a lot of phony cracks in that office, of all kinds and shapes, but that one by Henry

Jameson Heath took the cake. Staring at her, he said calmly, "I must do my duty as a citizen, Mrs. Rackell."

Wolfe spoke. "Archie, get Mr. Cramer."

I stepped to my desk and dialed.

IX

SATURDAY noon, the next day, Wengert and Cramer stood there in the office, at the end of Wolfe's desk. They were standing because, having been there nearly an hour and covered all the points, they were ready to leave. They had not admitted in so many words that Wolfe had done the American people, including them, a favor, but on the whole they had been sociable.

As they were turning to go I said, "Excuse me, one little thing."

They looked at me. I spoke to Wengert. "I thought Mr. Wolfe might mention it, but he didn't, and neither did you. I only bring it up to offer a constructive criticism. An FBI undercover girl, even one disguised as a Commie, shouldn't get in the habit of hurting people's feelings just for the hell of it. It didn't do a particle of good for Carol Berk to call me a crummy little stooge before a witness. Of course she was sore because I found her in the closet, but even so. I think you ought to speak to her about it."

Wengert was frowning at me. "Carol Berk? What kind of a gag is this?"

"Oh, come off it." I was disgusted. "How thick could I get? It was so obvious Mr. Wolfe didn't even bother to comment on it. Who else could have told you about my talk with Della Devlin? She trusted Miss Berk enough to let her hide in the closet, so of course she told her about it. Do you want to debate it with me on TV?"

"No. Nor with anybody else. You talk too damn much."

"Only with the right people. Say please, and I'll promise not to tell. I just wanted to make a helpful suggestion. I may be crummy and I may be a stooge, but I'm not little."

Cramer snorted. "If you ask me there's too much of you. About a hundred and eighty pounds too much. Come on, Wengert, I'm late."

They went. I supposed that was the last of that, but a couple of days later, Monday afternoon, while Wolfe was dictating a letter, the phone rang and a voice said it was Carol Berk. I said hello, showing no enthusiasm, and asked her, "How are your manners?"

"Rotten when required," she said cheerfully. "Privately like this, from a phone booth, I can be charming. I thought it was only fair for me to apologize for calling you little."

"Okay, go ahead."

"I thought you might prefer it face to face. I'm willing to take the trouble if you insist."

"Well, I'll tell you. I had an idea last week, Wednesday I think it was, that I ought to find time some day to tell you why I don't like you. We could meet and clean it up. I'll tell you why I don't like you, and you'll apologize. The Churchill bar at four-thirty? Can you be seen with me in public?"

"Certainly, I'm supposed to be seen in public."

"Fine. I'll have a hammer and sickle in my buttonhole."

As I hung up and swiveled I told Wolfe, "That was Carol Berk. I'm going to buy her a drink and possibly food. Since she was connected with the case we've just finished, of course I'll put it on the expense account."

"You will not," he asserted and resumed the dictation.

THE COP-KILLER

I

THERE were several reasons why I had no complaints as I walked along West Thirty-fifth Street that morning, approaching the stoop of Nero Wolfe's old brownstone house. The day was sunny and sparkling, my new shoes felt fine after the two-mile walk, a complicated infringement case had been polished off for a big client, and I had just deposited a check in five figures to Wolfe's account in the bank.

Five paces short of the stoop I became aware that two people, a man and a woman, were standing on the sidewalk across the street, staring either at the stoop or at me, or maybe both. That lifted me a notch higher, with the thought that while two rubbernecks might not put us in a class with the White House still it was nothing to sneeze at, until a second glance made me realize that I had seen them before. But where? Instead of turning up the steps I faced them, just as they stepped off the curb and started to me.

"Mr. Goodwin," the woman said in a sort of gasping whisper that barely reached me.

She was fair-skinned and blue-eyed, young enough, kind of nice-looking and neat in a dark blue assembly-line coat. He was as dark as she was fair, not much bigger than her, with his nose slanting slightly to the left and a full wide mouth. My delay in recognizing him was because I had never seen him with a hat on before. He was the hat-and-coat-and-tie custodian at the barber shop I went to.

"Oh, it's you, Carl—"

"Can we go in with you?" the woman asked in the same gasping whisper, and then I knew her too. She was also from the barber shop, a manicure. I had never hired her, since I do my own nails, but had seen her around and had heard her called Tina.

I looked down at her smooth white little face with its pointed chin and didn't care for the expression on it. I glanced at Carl, and he looked even worse.

"What's the matter?" I guess I was gruff. "Trouble?"

"Please not out here," Tina pleaded. Her eyes darted left and right and back up at me. "We just got enough brave to go to the door when you came. We were thinking which door, the one down below or up the steps. Please let us in?"

It did not suit my plans. I had counted on getting a few little chores done before Wolfe came down from the plant rooms at eleven o'clock. There could be no profit in this.

"You told me once," Carl practically whined, "that people in danger only have to mention your name."

"Nuts. A pleasantry. I talk too much." But I was stuck. "Okay, come in and tell me about it."

I led the way up the steps and let us in with my key. Inside, the first door on the left of the long wide hall was to what we called the front room, not much used, and I opened it, thinking to get it over with in there, but Fritz was there, dusting, so I took them along to the next door and on into the office. After moving a couple of chairs so they would be facing me I sat at my desk and nodded at them impatiently. Tina had looked around swiftly before she sat.

"Such a nice safe room," she said, "for you and Mr. Wolfe, two such great men."

"He's the great one," I corrected her. "I just caddy. What's this about danger?"

"We love this country," Carl said emphatically. All of a sudden he started trembling, first his hands, then his arms and shoulders, then all over. Tina darted to him and grabbed his elbows and shook him, not gently, and said things to him in some language I wasn't up on. He mumbled back at her and then got more vocal, and after a little the trembling stopped, and she returned to her chair.

"We do love this country," she declared.

I nodded. "Wait till you see Chillicothe, Ohio, where I was born. Then you *will* love it. How far west have you been, Tenth Avenue?"

"I don't think so." Tina was doubtful. "I think Eighth Avenue. But that's what we want to do, go west." She decided it would help to let me have a smile, but it didn't work too well. "We can't go east, can we, into the ocean?" She opened her blue leather handbag and, with no fingering or digging, took something from it. "But you see, we don't know where to go. This Ohio, maybe? I have fifty dollars here."

"That would get you there," I allowed.

She shook her head. "Oh, no. The fifty dollars is for you. You know our name, Vardas? You know we are married? So there is no question of morals, we are very high in morals, only all we want is to do our work and live in private, Carl and me, and we think—"

Having heard the clatter of Wolfe's elevator descending from the plant rooms on the roof, I had known an interruption was coming but had let her proceed. Now she stopped as Wolfe's steps sounded and he appeared at the door. Carl and Tina both bounced to their feet. Two paces in, after a quick glance at them, Wolfe stopped short and glowered at me.

"I didn't tell you we had callers," I said cheerfully, "because I knew you would be down soon. You know Carl, at the barber shop? And Tina, you've seen her there too. It's all right, they're married. They just dropped in to buy fifty bucks' worth of—"

Without a word or even a nod, Wolfe turned all of his seventh of a ton and beat it out and toward the door to the kitchen at the rear. The Vardas family stared at the doorway a moment and then turned to me.

"Sit down," I invited them. "As you said, he's a great

man. He's sore because I didn't notify him we had
company, and he was expecting to sit there behind his
desk"—I waved a hand—"and ring for beer and enjoy himself. He wouldn't wiggle a finger for fifty dollars. Maybe I
won't either, but let's see." I looked at Tina, who was back
on the edge of her chair. "You were saying . . ."

"We don't want Mr. Wolfe mad at us," she said in
distress.

"Forget it. He's only mad at me, which is chronic. What
do you want to go to Ohio for?"

"Maybe not Ohio." She tried to smile again. "It's what
I said, we love this country and we want to go more into
it—far in. We would like to be in the middle of it. We
want you to tell us where to go, to help us—"

"No, no." I was brusque. "Start from here. Look at you,
you're both scared stiff. What's the danger Carl mentioned?"

"I don't think," she protested, "it makes any difference—"

"That's no good," Carl said harshly. His hands started
trembling again, but he gripped the sides of his chair seat,
and they stopped. His dark eyes fastened on me. "I met
Tina," he said in a low level voice, trying to keep feeling
out of it, "three years ago in a concentration camp in
Russia. If you want me to I will tell you why it was that
they would never have let us get out of there alive, not in
one hundred years, but I would rather not talk so much
about it. It makes me start to tremble, and I am trying to
learn to act and talk of a manner so I can quit trembling."

I concurred. "Save it for some day after you stop
trembling. But you did get out alive?"

"Plainly. We are here." There was an edge of triumph
to the level voice. "I will not tell you about that either.
But they think we are dead. Of course Vardas was not our
name then, neither of us. We took that name later, when
we got married in Istanbul. Then we so managed—"

"You shouldn't tell any places," Tina scolded him. "No
places at all and no people at all."

"You are most right," Carl admitted. He informed me,
"It was not Istanbul."

I nodded. "Istanbul is out. You would have had to swim. You got married, that's the point."

"Yes. Then, later, we nearly got caught again. We did get caught, but—"

"No!" Tina said positively.

"Very well, Tina. You are most right. We went many other places, and at a certain time in a certain way we crossed the ocean. We had tried very hard to come to this country according to your rules, but it was in no way possible. When we did get into New York it was more by an accident—no, I did not say that. I will not say that much. Only I will say we got into New York. For a while it was so difficult, but it has been nearly a year now, since we got the jobs at the barber shop, that life has been so fine and sweet that we are almost healthy again. What we eat! We have even got some money saved! We have got—"

"Fifty dollars," Tina said hastily.

"Most right," Carl agreed. "Fifty American dollars. I can say as a fact that we would be healthy and happy beyond our utmost dreams three years ago, except for the danger. The danger is that we did not follow your rules. I will not deny that they are good rules, but for us they were impossible. We cannot expect ourselves to be happy when we don't know what minute someone may come and ask us how we got here. The minute that just went by, that was all right, no one asked, but here is the next minute. Every day is full of those minutes, so many. We have found a way to learn what would happen, and we know where we would be sent back to. We know exactly what would happen to us. I would not be surprised if you felt a deep contempt when you saw me trembling the way I do, but to understand a situation like this I believe you have to be somewhat close to it. As I am. As Tina is. I am not saying you would tremble like me—after all, Tina never does— but I think you might have your own way of showing that you were not really happy."

"Yeah, I might," I agreed. I glanced at Tina, but the expression on her face could have made me uncomfortable, so I looked back at Carl. "But if I tried to figure a way out I doubt if I would pick on spilling it to a guy named Archie

Goodwin just because he came to the barber shop where I worked. He might be crazy about the rules you couldn't follow, and anyhow there are just as many minutes in Ohio as there are in New York."

"There is that fifty dollars." Carl extended his hands, not trembling, toward me.

Tina gestured impatiently. "That's nothing to you," she said, letting bitterness into it for the first time. "We know that, it's nothing. But the danger has come, and we had to have someone tell us where to go. This morning a man came to the barber shop and asked us questions. An official! A policeman!"

"Oh." I glanced from one to the other. "That's different. A policeman in uniform?"

"No, in regular clothes, but he showed us a card in a case, New York Police Department. His name was on it, Jacob Wallen."

"What time this morning?"

"A little after nine o'clock, soon after the shop was open. He talked first with Mr. Fickler, the owner, and Mr. Fickler brought him around behind the partition to my booth, where I do customers when they're through in the chair or when they only want a manicure, and I was there, getting things together, and he sat down and took out a notebook and asked me questions. Then he—"

"What kind of questions?"

"All about me. My name, where I live, where I came from, how long I've been working there, all that kind, and then about last night, where I was and what I was doing last night."

"Did he say why he was curious about last night?"

"No. He just asked questions."

"What part of last night did he ask about? All of it?"

"Yes, from the time the shop closes, half-past six, from then on."

"Where did you tell him you came from?"

"I said Carl and I are DPs from Italy. That's what we had decided to say. We have to say something when people are just curious."

"I suppose you do. Did he ask to see your papers?"

"No. That will come next." She set her jaw. "We can't go back there. We have to leave New York today—now."

"What else did he ask?"

"That's all. It was mostly about last night."

"Then what? Did he question Carl too?"

"Yes, but not right after me. He sent me away, and Mr. Fickler sent Philip to him in the booth, and when Philip came out he sent Carl in, and when Carl came out he sent Jimmie in. Jimmie was still in the booth with him when I went to Carl, up front by the rack, and we knew we had to get out. We waited until Mr. Fickler had gone to the back of the shop for something, and then we just walked out. We went to our room down on the East Side and packed our stuff and started for Grand Central with it, and then we realized we didn't know anything about where to go and might make some terrible mistake, so there in Grand Central we talked it over. We decided that since the police were after us already it couldn't be any worse, but we weren't sure enough about any of the people we have met in New York, so the best thing would be to come to you and pay you to help us. You're a professional detective, and anyway Carl likes you about the best of all the customers. You only tip him a dime, so it's not that. I have noticed you myself, the way you look. You look like a man who would break rules too—if you had to."

I gave her a sharp look, suspicious, but if she was trying to butter me she was very good. All that showed in her blue eyes was the scare that had put them on the run and the hope of me they were hanging on to for dear life. I looked at Carl. The scare was there too, but I couldn't see the hope. Still he sat solid on the chair, with no sign of trembling, as I thought to myself that it would have been no surprise to him if I had picked up the phone and called the cops. Either he had his full share of guts or he had run out entirely.

I was irritated. "Damn it," I protested, "you bring it here already broke. What did you beat it for? That alone fixes you. He was questioning the others too and he was concentrating on last night. What about last night? What were you doing, breaking some more rules?"

They both started to answer, but she let him take it. He said no, they weren't. They had gone straight home from work and eaten in their room as usual. Tina had washed some clothes, and Carl had read a book. Around nine they had gone for a walk, and had been back in their room and in bed before ten-thirty.

I was disgusted. "You sure did it up," I declared. "If you're clean for last night, why didn't you stay put? You must have something in your heads or you wouldn't have stayed alive and got this far. Why didn't you use it?"

Carl smiled at me. He really did smile, but it didn't make me want to smile back. "A policeman asking questions," he said in the level tone he had used before, "has a different effect on different people. If you have a country like this one and you are innocent of crime, all the people of your country are saying it with you when you answer the questions. That is true even when you are away from home—especially when you are away from home. But Tina and I have no country at all. The country we had once, it is no longer a country, it is just a place to wait to die, only if we are sent back there we will not have to wait. Two people alone cannot answer a policeman's questions anywhere in the world. It takes a whole country to speak to a policeman, and Tina and I—we do not have one."

"You see," Tina said. "Here, take it." She got up and came to me, extending a hand with the money in it. "Take it, Mr. Goodwin! Just tell us where to go, all the little facts that will help us—"

"Or we thought," Carl suggested, not hopefully, "that you might give us a letter to some friend, in this Ohio perhaps—not that we should expect too much for fifty dollars."

I looked at them, with my lips pressed together. The morning was shot now anyway, with Wolfe sore and my chores not done. I swiveled to my desk and picked up the phone. Any one of three or four city employees would probably find out for me what kind of errand had taken a dick named Wallen to the Goldenrod Barber Shop, unless it was something very special. But with my finger in the dial hole I hesitated and then replaced the phone. If it was something hot I would be starting PD cars for our address, and Wolfe and I both have a prejudice against cops yanking people out of his office, no matter who they are, unless we ourselves have got them ready for delivery. So I swiveled again. Carl was frowning at me, his head moving from side to side. Tina was standing tense, the money clutched in her fist.

"This is silly," I said. "If they're really after you, you'd be throwing your money away on carfare to Ohio or anywhere else. Save it for a lawyer. I'll have to go up there and see what it's all about." I got up, crossed to the sound-proof door to the front room, and opened it. "You can wait here. In here, please."

"We'll go," Tina said, back to her gasping whisper again. "We won't bother you any more. Come, Carl—"

"Skip it," I said curtly. "If this amounts to anything more than petty larceny you'd be nabbed sure as hell. This is my day for breaking a rule, and I'll be back soon. Come on, I'll put you in here, and I advise you to stay put."

They looked at each other.

"I like him," Carl said.

Tina moved. She came and passed through into the front room, and Carl was right behind her.

I told them to sit down and relax and not get restless, shut the door, went to the kitchen, where Wolfe was seated at the far end of the long table, drinking beer, and told him, "The check from Pendexter came and has been deposited. That pair of foreigners have got themselves in a mess. I put them in the front room and told them to stay there until I get back."

"Where are you going?" he demanded.

"A little detective work, not in your class. I won't be gone long. You can dock me."

I left.

II

THE Goldenrod Barber Shop was in the basement of an office building on Lexington Avenue in the upper Thirties. I had been patronizing one of the staff, named Ed, for several years. Formerly, from away back, Wolfe had gone to an artist in a shop on Twenty-eighth Street, named Fletcher. When Fletcher had retired a couple of years ago Wolfe had switched to Goldenrod and tried my man, Ed, hadn't liked him, had experimented with the rest of the Goldenrod staff, and had settled on Jimmie. His position now, after two years, was that Jimmie was no Fletcher, especially with a shampoo, but that he was some better than tolerable.

Goldenrod, with only six chairs and usually only four of them manned, and two manicures, was no Framinelli's, but it was well equipped and clean, and anyhow it had Ed, who was a little rough at tilting a head maybe but knew exactly how to handle my hair and had a razor so sharp and slick you never knew it was on you.

I hadn't shaved that morning and as, at noon, I paid the taxi driver, entered the building, and descended the stairs to the basement, my plan of campaign was simple. I would get in Ed's chair, waiting if necessary, and ask him to give me a once-over, and the rest would be easy.

But it was neither simple nor easy. A medium-sized mob of white-collar workers, buzzing and chattering, was ranged three deep along the wall of the corridor facing the door of the shop. Others, passing by in both directions, were stopping to try to look in, and a flatfoot, posted in the doorway, was telling them to keep moving. That did not look promising, or else it did, if that's how you like things. I swerved aside and halted for a survey through the open door and the glass. Joel Fickler, the boss, was at the rack where Carl usually presided, taking a man's coat to put on a hanger. A man with his hat on was backed up to the cashier's counter, with his elbows on it, facing the

64

whole shop. Two other men with their hats on were seated near the middle of the row of chairs for waiting customers, one of them next to the little table for magazines. They were discussing something without much enthusiasm. Two of the barbers' chairs, Ed's and Tom's, were occupied. The other two barbers, Jimmie and Philip, were on their stools against the wall. Janet, the other manicure, was not in sight.

I stepped to the doorway and was going on in. The flatfoot blocked me.

I lifted my brows at him. "What's all the excitement?"

"Accident in here. No one allowed in."

"How did the customers in the chairs get in? I'm a customer."

"Only customers with appointments. You got one?"

"Certainly." I stuck my head through the doorway and yelled, "Ed! How soon?"

The man leaning on the counter straightened up and turned for a look. At sight of me he grunted. "I'll be damned. Who whistled for you?"

The presence of my old friend and enemy Sergeant Purley Stebbins of Manhattan Homicide gave the thing an entirely different flavor. Up to then I had just been mildly curious, floating along. Now all my nerves and muscles snapped to attention. Sergeant Stebbins is not interested in petty larceny. I didn't care for the possibility of having shown a pair of murderers to chairs in our front room.

"Good God," Purley grumbled, "is this going to turn into one of them Nero Wolfe babies?"

"Not unless you turn it." I grinned at him. "Whatever it is, I dropped in for a shave, that's all, and here you boys are, to my surprise." The flatfoot had given me leeway, and I had crossed the sill. "I'm a regular customer here." I turned to Fickler, who had trotted over to us. "How long have I been leaving my hair here, Joel?"

None of Fickler's bones were anywhere near the surface except on his bald head. He was six inches shorter than me, which may have been one reason why I had never got a straight look into his narrow black eyes. He had never liked me much since the day he had forgotten to list an appointment with Ed I had made on the phone, and I, under provocation, had made a few pointed remarks. Now he looked as if he had been annoyed by something much worse than remarks.

"Over six years, Mr. Goodwin," he said. "This," he told Purley, "is the famous detective, Mr. Archie Goodwin. Mr. Nero Wolfe comes here too."

"The hell he does." Purley, scowling at me, said in a certain tone, "Famous."

I shrugged. "Just a burden. A damn nuisance."

"Yeah. Don't let it get you down. You just dropped in for a shave?"

"Yes, sir. Write it down, and I'll sign it."

"Who's your barber?"

"Ed."

"That's Graboff. He's busy."

"So I see. I'm not pressed. I'll chat with you or read a magazine or get a manicure."

"I don't feel like chatting." Purley had not relaxed the scowl. "You know a guy that works here named Carl Vardas? And his wife, Tina, a manicure?"

"I know Carl well enough to pay him a dime for my hat and coat and tie. I can't say I know Tina, but of course I've seen her here. Why?"

"I'm just asking. There's no law against your coming here for a shave, since you need one and this is where you come, but the sight of either you or Wolfe makes me want to scratch. No wonder, huh? So to have it on the record in case it's needed, have you seen Vardas or his wife this morning?"

"Sure I have." I stretched my neck to get closer to his ear and whispered, "I put them in our front room and told them to wait, and beat it up here to tell you, and if you'll step on it—"

"I don't care for gags," he growled. "Not right now. They killed a cop, or one of them did. You know how much we like that."

I did indeed and adjusted my face accordingly. "The hell they did. One of yours? Did I know him?"

"No. A dick from the Twentieth Precinct, Jake Wallen."

"Where and when?"

"This morning, right here. The other side of that partition, in her manicure booth. Stuck a long pair of scissors in his back and got his pump. Apparently he never made a sound, but them massage things are going here off and on. By the time he was found they had gone. It took us an hour to find out where they lived, and when we got there they had been and got their stuff and beat it."

I grunted sympathetically. "Is it tied up? Prints on the scissors or something?"

"We'll do all right without prints," Purley said grimly. "Didn't I say they lammed?"

"Yes, but," I objected, not aggressively, "some people can get awful scared at sight of a man with scissors sticking in his back. I wasn't intimate with Carl, but he didn't strike me as a man who would stab a cop just on principle. Was Wallen here to take him?"

Purley's reply was stopped before it got started. Tom had finished with his customer, and the two men with hats on in the row of chairs ranged along the partition were keeping their eyes on the customer as he went to the rack for his tie. Tom, having brushed himself off, had walked to the front and up to us. Usually Tom bounced around like a high-school kid—from his chair to the wall cabinet and back again, or over to the steamer behind the partition for a hot towel—in spite of his white-haired sixty-some years, but today his feet dragged. Nor did he tell me hello, though he gave me a sort of a glance before he spoke to Purley.

"It's my lunchtime, Sergeant. I just go to the cafeteria at the end of the hall."

Purley called a name that sounded like Joffe, and one of the dicks on a chair by the partition got up and came.

"Yerkes is going to lunch," Purley told him. "Go along and stay with him."

"I want to phone my wife," Tom said resolutely.

"Why not? Stay with him, Joffe."

"Yes, sir."

They went, with Tom in front. Purley and I moved out of the way as the customer approached to pay his check and Fickler sidled around behind the cash register.

"I thought," I said politely, "you had settled for Carl and Tina. Why does Tom have to have company at lunch?"

"We haven't got Carl and Tina."

"But you soon will have, the way the personnel feels about cop-killers. Why pester these innocent barbers? If one of them gets nervous and slices a customer, then what?"

Purley merely snarled.

I stiffened. "Excuse me. I'm not so partial to cop-killers either. It seemed only natural to show some interest. Luckily I can read, so I'll catch it in the evening paper."

"Don't bust a gut." Purley's eyes were following the customer as he walked to the door and on out past the flat-foot. "Sure we'll get Carl and Tina, but if you don't mind we'll just watch these guys' appetites. You asked what Jake Wallen was here for."

"I asked if he came to take Carl."

"Yeah. I think he did but I can't prove it yet. Last night around midnight a couple of pedestrians, two women, were hit by a car at Eighty-first and Broadway. Both killed. The car kept going. It was found later parked at Ninety-sixth and Broadway, just across from the subway entrance. We haven't found anyone who saw the driver, either at the scene of the accident or where the car was parked. The car was hot. It had been parked by its owner at eight o'clock on Forty-eighth Street between Ninth and Tenth, and was gone when he went for it at eleven-thirty."

Purley paused to watch a customer enter. The customer got past the flatfoot with Joel Fickler's help, left things at the rack, and went and got on Jimmie's chair. Purley returned to me. "When the car was spotted by a squad car at Ninety-sixth and Broadway with a dented fender and blood and other items that tagged it, the Twentieth Precinct sent Jake Wallen to it. He was the first one to give it a look. Later, of course, there was a gang from all over, including the laboratory, before they moved it. Wallen was supposed to go home and to bed at eight in the morning when his trick ended, but he didn't. He phoned his wife that he had a hot lead on a hit-and-run killer and was going to handle it himself and grab a promotion. Not only that, he phoned the owner of the car at his home in Yonkers, and asked him if he had any connection with the Goldenrod Barber Shop or knew anyone who had, or if he had ever been there. The owner had never heard of it. Of course we've collected all this since we were called here at ten-fifteen and found Wallen DOA with scissors in his back."

I was frowning. "But what gave him the lead to this shop?"

"We'd like to know. It had to be something he found in the car, we don't know what. The goddam fool kept it to himself and came here and got killed."

"Didn't he show it or mention it to anyone here?"

"They say not. All he had with him was a newspaper. We've got it—today's News, the early, out last night. We can't spot anything in it. There was nothing in his pockets, nothing on him, that helps any."

I humphed. "Fool is right. Even if he had cleaned it up he wouldn't have grabbed a promotion. He would have been more apt to grab a uniform and a beat."

"Yeah, he was that kind. There's too many of that kind. Not to mention names, but these precinct men—"

A phone rang. Fickler, by the cash register, looked at Purley, who stepped to the counter where the phone was and answered the call. It was for him. When, after a minute, it seemed to be going on, I moved away and had gone a few paces when a voice came.

"Hello, Mr. Goodwin."

It was Jimmie, Wolfe's man, using comb and scissors above his customer's right ear. He was the youngest of the staff, about my age, and by far the handsomest, with curly lips and white teeth and dancing dark eyes. I had never understood why he wasn't at Framinelli's. I told him hello.

"Mr. Wolfe ought to be here," he said.

Under the circumstances I thought that a little tactless,

and was even prepared to tell him so when Ed called to me from two chairs down. "Fifteen minutes, Mr. Goodwin? All right?"

I told him okay, I would wait, went to the rack and undressed to my shirt, and crossed to one of the chairs over by the partition, next to the table with magazines. I thought it would be fitting to pick up a magazine, but I had already read the one on top, the latest *New Yorker*, and the one on top on the shelf below was the *Time* of two weeks ago. So I leaned back and let my eyes go, slow motion, from left to right and back again. Though I had been coming there for six years I didn't really know those people, in spite of the reputation barbers have as conversationalists. I knew that Fickler, the boss, had once been attacked bodily there in the shop by his ex-wife; that Philip had had two sons killed in World War II; that Tom had once been accused by Fickler of swiping lotions and other supplies and had slapped Fickler's face; that Ed played the horses and was always in debt; that Jimmie had to be watched or he would take magazines from the shop while they were still current; and that Janet, who had only been there a year, was suspected of having a sideline, maybe dope peddling. Aside from such items as those, they were strangers.

Suddenly Janet was there in front of me. She had come from around the end of the partition, and not alone. The man with her was a broad-shouldered husky, gray-haired and gray-eyed, with an unlit cigar slanting up from a corner of his mouth. His eyes swept the whole shop, and since he started at the far right he ended up at me.

He stared. "For God's sake," he muttered. "You? Now what?"

I was surprised for a second to see Inspector Cramer himself, head of Manhattan Homicide, there on the job. But even an inspector likes to be well thought of by the rank and file, and here it was no mere citizen who had met his end but one of them. The whole force would appreciate it. Besides, I have to admit he's a good cop.

"Just waiting for a shave," I told him. "I'm an old customer here. Ask Purley."

Purley came over and verified me, but Cramer checked with Ed himself. Then he drew Purley aside, and they mumbled back and forth a while, after which Cramer summoned Philip and escorted him around the end of the partition.

Janet seated herself in the chair next to mine. She looked even better in profile than head on, with her nice chin and straight little nose and long home-grown lashes. I felt a little in debt to her for the mild pleasure I had got occasionally as I sat in Ed's chair and glanced at her while she worked on the customer in the next chair.

"I was wondering where you were," I remarked.

She turned to me. She wasn't old enough to have wrinkles or seams but she looked old enough then. She was putting a strain on every muscle in her face, and it certainly showed.

"Did you say something?" she asked.

"Nothing vital. My name's Goodwin. Call me Archie."

"I know. You're a detective. How can I keep them from having my picture in the paper?"

"You can't if they've already got it. Have they?"

"I think so. I wish I was dead."

"I don't." I made it not loud but emphatic.

"Why should you? I do. My folks in Michigan think I'm acting or modeling. I leave it vague. And here—oh, my God."

Her chin worked, but she controlled it.

"Work is work," I said. "My parents wanted me to be a college president, and I wanted to be a second baseman, and look at me. Anyhow, if your picture gets printed and it's a good likeness, who knows what will happen?"

"This is my Gethsemane," she said.

That made me suspicious, naturally. She had mentioned acting. "Come off it," I advised her. "Think of someone else. Think of the guy that got stabbed—no, he's out of it—think of his wife, how do you suppose she feels? Or Inspector Cramer, with the job he's got. What was he asking you just now?"

She didn't hear me. She said through clamped teeth, "I only wish I had some guts."

"Why? What would you do?"

"I'd tell all about it."

"All about what?"

"About what happened."

"You mean last night? Why not try it out on me and see how it goes? That doesn't take guts, just go ahead and let it come, keep your voice down and let it flow."

She didn't hear a word. Her ears were disconnected. She kept her brown eyes, under the long lashes, straight at me.

"How it happened this morning. How I was going back to my booth after I finished Mr. Levinson in Philip's chair, and he called me into Tina's booth and he seized me, with one hand on my throat so I couldn't scream, and there was no doubt at all what he intended, so I grabbed the scissors from the shelf and, without realizing what I was doing, plunged them into him with all my strength, and his grip on me loosened, and he collapsed onto the chair. That's what I would do if I had any guts and if I really want a successful career the way I say I do. I would have to be arrested and have a trial, and then—"

"Hold it. Your pronouns. Mr. Levinson called you into Tina's booth?"

"Certainly not. That man that got killed." She tilted her head back. "See the marks on my throat?"

There was no mark whatever on her smooth pretty throat.

"Good Lord," I said. "That would get you top billing anywhere."

"That's what I was saying."

"Then go ahead and tell it."

"I can't! I simply can't! It would be so darned vulgar."

Her full face was there, only sixteen inches away, with the muscles no longer under strain, the closest I had ever been to it, and there was no question about how lovely it was. Under different circumstances my reaction would have been merely normal and healthy, but at the moment I could have slapped it with pleasure. I had felt a familiar tingle at the base of my spine when I thought she was going to open up about a midnight ride up Broadway, probably with one of her co-workers, possibly with the boss himself, and then she had danced off into this folderol.

She needed a lesson. "I understand your position," I said, "a girl as sweet and fine and strong as you, but it's bound to come out in the end, and I want to help. Incidentally, I am not married. I'll go to Inspector Cramer right now and tell him about it. He'll want to take photographs of your throat. I know the warden down at the jail and I'll see that you get good treatment, no rough stuff. Do you know any lawyers?"

She shook her head, answering, I thought, my question about lawyers, but no. She didn't believe in answering questions. "About your being married," she said, " I hadn't even thought. There was an article in the *American* magazine last month about career girls getting married. Did you read it?"

"No. I may be able to persuade the district attorney to make it a manslaughter charge instead of murder, which would please your folks in Michigan." I drew my feet back and slid forward on the chair, ready to rise. "Okay, I'll go tell Cramer."

"That article was silly," she said. "I think a girl must get her career established *first*. That's why when I see an attractive man I never wonder if he's married; by the time I'm ready for one these will be too old. That's why I wouldn't ask you if you know anyone in show business, because I wouldn't take help from a man. I think a girl—"

If Ed hadn't signaled to me just then, his customer having left the chair, there's no telling how it would have ended. It would have been vulgar to slap her, and no words would have been any good since she was deaf, but surely I might have thought of somthing that would have taken effect. As it was, I didn't want to keep Ed waiting so I got up and crossed to his chair and climbed in.

"Just scrape the face," I told him.

He got a bib on me and tilted me back. "Did you phone?" he asked. "Did that fathead forget again?"

I told him no, that I had been caught midtown with a stubble and an unforeseen errand for which I should be presentable and added, "You seem to have had some excitement."

He went to the cabinet for a tube of prefabricated lather, got some on me, and started rubbing. "We sure did," he said with feeling. "Carl, you know Carl, he killed a man in Tina's booth. Then they both ran. I'm sorry for Tina, she was all right, but Carl, I don't know." He moved to my left cheek.

I couldn't articulate with him rubbing. He finished, went to wipe his fingers, and came with the razor. I rolled my head into position, to the left, and remarked, "I'd sort of watch it, Ed. It's a little risky to go blabbing that Carl killed him unless you can prove it."

"Well, he had fits." The razor was as sharp and slick as usual. "What did he run for?"

"I couldn't say. But the cops are still poking around here, even an inspector."

"Sure they are, they're after evidence. You gotta have evidence." Ed pulled the skin tight over the jawbone. "For instance, they ask me did he show me anything or ask me anything about some article from the shop. I say he didn't. That would be evidence, see?"

"Yes, I get it." I could only mumble. "What did he ask you?"

"Oh, all about me, name, married or single—you know, insurance men, income tax, they all ask the same things. But when he asked about last night I told him where to get off, but then I thought what the hell and told him. Why not? That's my philosophy, Mr. Goodwin—why not? It saves trouble."

He was prying my chin up, doing the throat. That clean, I rolled my head to the right to turn the other cheek.

"Of course," he said, "the police have to get it straight, but they can't expect us to remember everything. When he came in first he talked with Fickler, maybe five minutes. Then Fickler took him to Tina's booth, and he talked with Tina. After that Fickler sent Philip in, and then Carl and then Jimmie and then Tom and then me and then Janet. I think it's pretty good to remember that."

I mumbled agreement. He was at the corner of my mouth.

"But I can't remember everything, and they can't make

me. I don't know how long it was after Janet came back out before Fickler went to Tina's booth and found him dead. They ask me was it nearer ten minutes or nearer fifteen, but I say I had a customer at the time, we all did but Philip, and I don't know. They ask me how many of us went behind the partition after Janet came out, to the steamer or the vat or to get the lamp or something, but I say again I had a customer at the time, and I don't know, except I know I didn't go because I was trimming Mr. Howell at the time. I was working the top when Fickler yelled and came running out. They can ask Mr. Howell."

"They probably have," I said, but to no one, because Ed had gone for a hot towel.

He returned and used the towel and got the lilac water. Patting it on, he resumed, "They ask me exactly when Carl and Tina went, they ask me that twenty times, but I can't say and I won't say. Carl did it all right, but they can't prove it by me. They've gotta have evidence, but I don't. Cold towel today?"

"No, I'll keep the smell."

He patted me dry, levered me upright, and brought a comb and brush. "Can I remember what I don't know?" he demanded.

"I know I can't."

"And I'm no great detective like you." Ed was a little rough with a brush. "And now I go for lunch but I've got to have a cop along. We can't even go to the can alone. They searched all of us down to the skin, and they even brought a woman to search Janet. They took our finger-prints. I admit they've gotta have evidence." He flipped the bib off. "How was the razor, all right?"

I told him it was fine as usual, stepped down, fished for a quarter, and exchanged it for my check. Purley Stebbins, nearby, was watching both of us. There had been times when I had seen fit to kid Purley at the scene of a murder, but not now. A cop had been killed.

He spoke, not belligerently. "The inspector don't like your being here."

"Neither do I," I declared. "Thank God this didn't happen to be Mr. Wolfe's day for a haircut, you would never have believed it. I'm just a minor coincidence. Nice to see you."

I went and paid my check to Fickler, got my things on, and departed.

III

A s I emerged into Lexington Avenue there were several things on my mind. The most immediate was this: if Cramer's suspicion had been aroused enough to spend a man on me, and if I were seen going directly home from the shop, there might be too much curiosity as to why I had chosen to spend six bits for a shave at that time of day. So instead of taking a taxi, which would have had to crawl crosstown anyhow, I walked, and when I got to Altman's I used their aisles and exits to make sure I had no tail. That left my mind free for other things the rest of the way home.

One leading question was whether Carl and Tina would still be where I had left them, in the front room. That was what took me up the seven steps of the stoop two at a time, and on in quick. The answer to the question was no. The front room was empty.

I strode down the hall to the office but stopped there because I heard Wolfe's voice. It was coming through the open door to the dining room, across the hall, and it was saying, "No, Mr. Vardas, I cannot agree that mountain climbing is merely one manifestation of man's spiritual aspirations. I think instead it is an hysterical paroxysm of his infantile vanity. One of the prime ambitions of a jack-ass is to bray louder than any other jackass, and man is not . . ."

I crossed the hall and the dining-room sill. Wolfe was at his end of the table, and Fritz, standing at his elbow, had just removed the lid from a steaming platter. At his left was Tina, and Carl was at his right, my place when there was no company. Wolfe saw me but finished his paragraph on mountain climbing before attending to me.

"In time, Archie. You like veal and mushrooms."

Talk about infantile. His not being willing to sit to his lunch with unfed people in the house was all well enough, but why not send trays in to them? That was easy—he was sore at me, and I had called them foreigners.

I stepped to the end of the table and said, "I know you have a paroxysm if I try to bring up business during meals, but eighteen thousand cops would give a month's pay to get their hands on Carl and Tina, your guests."

"Indeed." Wolfe was serving the veal and accessories. "Why?"

"Have you talked with them?"

"No. I merely invited them to lunch."

"Then don't until I've reported. I ran into Cramer and Stebbins at the barber shop."

"Confound it." The serving spoon stopped en route.

"Yeah. It's quite interesting. But first lunch, of course. I'll go put the chain bolt on. Please dish me some veal?"

Carl and Tina were speechless.

That lunch was one of Wolfe's best performances; I admit it. He didn't know a damn thing about Carl and Tina except that they were in a jam, he knew that Cramer and Stebbins dealt only with homicide, and he had a strong prejudice against entertaining murderers at his table. Some years back a female prospective client had dined with us in an emergency, on roast Watertown goose. It turned out that she was a husband-poisoner, and roast goose had been off our menu for a solid year, though Wolfe was very fond of it. His only hope now was his knowledge that I was aware of his prejudice and even shared it, and I took my seat at the end of the table and disposed of a big helping of the veal and mushrooms, followed by pumpkin puffs, without batting an eye. He must have been fairly tight inside, but he stayed the polite host clear to the end, with no sign of hurry even with the coffee. Then, however, the tension began to tell. Ordinarily his return to the office after a meal was leisurely and lazy, but this time he went right along, followed by his guests and me. He marched across to his chair behind the desk, got his bulk deposited, and snapped at me, "What have you got us into now?"

I was pulling chairs around so the Vardas family would be facing him, but stopped to give him an eye.

"Us?" I inquired.

"Yes."

"Okay," I said courteously, "if that's how it is. I did not invite them to come here, let alone to lunch. They came on their own, and I let them in, which is one of my functions. Having started it, I'll finish it. May I use the front room, please? I'll have them out of here in ten minutes."

"Pfui." He was supercilious. "I am now responsible for their presence, since they were my guests at lunch. Sit down, sir. Sit down, Mrs. Vardas, please."

Carl and Tina didn't know what from which. I had to push the chairs up behind their knees. Then I went to my own chair and swiveled to face Wolfe.

"I have a question to ask them," I told him, "but first you need a couple of facts. They're in this country without papers. They were in a concentration camp in Russia and they're not telling how they got here if they can help it. They could be spies, but I doubt it after hearing them talk. Naturally they jump a mile if they hear someone say boo, and when a man came to the barber shop this morning and showed a police card and asked who they were and where they came from and what they were doing last night they scooted the first chance they got. But they didn't know where to go so they came here to buy fifty bucks' worth of advice and information. I got bighearted and went to the shop disguised as a Boy Scout."

"You went?" Tina gasped.

I turned to them. "Sure I went. It's a complicated situation, and you made it worse by beating it, but you did and here we are. I think I can handle it if you two can be kept out of the way. It would be dangerous for you to stay here. I know a safe place up in the Bronx for you to lay low for a few days. You shouldn't take a chance on a taxi or the subway, so we'll go around the corner to the garage and get Mr. Wolfe's car, and you can drive it up there. Then I'll—"

"Excuse me," Carl said urgently. "You would drive us up there?"

"No, I'll be busy. Then I'll—"

"But I can't drive a car! I don't know how!"

"Then your wife will drive. You can leave—"

"She can't! She don't know either!"

I sprang from my chair and stood over them. "Look," I said savagely, "save that for the cops. Can't drive a car? Certainly you can! Everybody can!"

They were looking up at me, Carl bewildered, Tina frowning. "In America, yes," she said. "But we are not Americans, not yet. We have never had a chance to learn."

"You have never driven a car?"

"No. Never."

"And Carl?"

"Never."

"What the devil is this?" Wolfe demanded.

I returned to my chair. "That," I said, "was the question I wanted to ask. It has a bearing, as you'll soon see." I regarded Carl and Tina. "If you're lying about this, not knowing how to drive a car, you won't be sent back home to die, you'll die right here. It will be a cinch to find out if you're lying."

"Why should we?" Carl demanded. "What is so important in it?"

"Once more," I insisted. "Can you drive a car?"

"No."

"Can you, Tina?"

"No!"

"Okay." I turned to Wolfe. "The caller at the barber shop this morning was a precinct dick named Wallen. Fickler took him to Tina's booth, and he questioned Tina first. Then the others had sessions with him in the booth, in this order: Philip, Carl, Jimmie, Tom, Ed, and Janet. You may not know that the manicure booths are around behind the long partition. After Janet came out there was a period of ten or fifteen minutes when Wallen was in the booth alone. Then Fickler went to see, and what he saw was Wallen's body with scissors buried in his back. Someone had stabbed him to death. Since Carl and Tina had lammed—"

Tina's cry was more of a gasp, a last gasp, an awful sound. With one leap she was out of her chair and at Carl, grasping him and begging wildly, "Carl, no! No, no! Oh, Carl—"

"Make her stop," Wolfe snapped.

I had to try, because Wolfe would rather be in a room with a hungry tiger than with a woman out of hand. I went and got a grip on her shoulder but released it at sight of the expression on Carl's face as he pushed to his feet against her pressure. It looked as if he could and would handle it. He did. He straightened her up, standing against her, his face nearly touching hers, and told her, "No! Do you understand? No!"

He eased her back to her chair and down onto it, and turned to me. "That man was killed there in Tina's booth?"

"Yes."

Carl smiled as he had once before, and I wished he would stop trying it. "Then of course," he said as if he were conceding a point in a tight argument, "this is the end for us. But please I must ask you not to blame my wife. Because we have been through many things together she is ready to credit me with many deeds that are far beyond me. She has a big idea of me, and I have a big idea of her. But I did not kill that man. I did not touch him." He frowned. "I don't understand why you suggested riding in a car to the Bronx. Of course you will give us to the police."

"Forget the Bronx." I was frowning back. "Every cop in town has his eye peeled for you. Sit down."

He stood. He looked at Tina, at Wolfe, and back down at me.

"Sit down, damn it!"

He went to his chair and sat.

"About driving a car," Wolfe muttered. "Was that flummery?"

"No, sir, that comes next. Last night around midnight a hit-and-run driver in a stolen car killed two women up on Broadway. The car was found parked at Broadway and Ninety-sixth Street. Wallen, from the Twentieth Precinct, was the first dick to look it over. In it he apparently found something that led him to the Goldenrod Barber Shop—anyhow he phoned his wife that he was on a hot one that would lead to glory and a raise and then he showed up at the shop and called the roll, as described. With the result also as described. Cramer has bought it that the hit-and-run driver found himself cornered and used the scissors, and Cramer, don't quote me, is not a dope. To qualify as a hit-and-run driver you must meet certain specifications, and one of them is knowing how to drive a car. So the best plan would be for Carl and Tina to go back to the shop and report for duty and for the official quiz, if it wasn't for two things. First, the fact that they lammed will make it very tough, and second, even though it is settled that they didn't kill a cop, their lack of documents will fix them anyhow."

I waved a hand. "So actually what's the difference? If they're sent back where they came from they're doomed there, that's all they have to pick from. One interesting angle is that you are harboring fugitives from justice, and I am not. I told Purley they're here. So you're—"

"You what?" Wolfe bellowed.

"What I said. That's the advantage of having a reputation for gags, you can say practically anything if you handle your face right. I told him they were here in our front room, and he sailed right over it. So I'm clean, but you're not. You can't even just show them out. If you don't want to call Cramer yourself, which I admit would be a little thick since they were your luncheon guests, I could get Purley at the shop and tell him they're still here and why hasn't he sent for them."

"It might be better," Tina said, not with hope, "just a little better, if you would let us go ourselves? No?"

She got no answer. Wolfe was glaring at me. It wasn't that he needed my description of the situation to realize what a pickle he was in; I have never tried to deny that the interior decorator did a snappier job inside his skull than in mine. What had him boiling was my little stunt of get-

ting it down that neither Carl nor Tina could drive a car.
But for that it would still have been possible to let them
meet the law and take what they got, and more or less
shrug it off; now that was out of the question. Also, naturally, he resented my putting the burden on him. If I had
taken a stand as a champion of humanity he could have
blamed me for any trouble he was put to—and didn't I
know he would.

"There is," he said, glaring, "another alternative to consider."

"Yes, sir. What?"

"Let us just go ourselves," Tina said.

"Pfui." He moved the glare to her. "You would try to
skedaddle and be caught within an hour." Back to me.
"You have told Mr. Stebbins they are here. We can simply
keep them here and await developments. Since Mr. Cramer
and Mr. Stebbins are still there at work, they may at any
moment disclose the murderer."

"Sure they may," I agreed, "but I doubt it. They're just
being thorough; they've really settled for Carl and Tina,
and what they're looking for is evidence, especially what
it was that led Wallen to the barber shop—though I suppose they haven't much hope of that, since Carl and Tina
could have taken it along. Anyway, you know how it is
when they've got their minds aimed in one direction."

Wolfe's eyes went to Carl. "Did you and your wife leave
the shop together?"

Carl shook his head. "That might have been noticed, so
she went first. There is no place for ladies to go in the shop,
so Tina and the other girl, Janet, go to a place down the
hall when they need to, and she could leave with no attention. When she was gone I waited until they were all busy
and Mr. Fickler was walking behind the partition, then I
went quick out the door and ran upstairs to meet her
there."

"When was that?" I asked. "Who was in Tina's booth
with Wallen?"

"I don't think anybody was. Janet had come out a while
before. She was at Jimmie's chair with a customer."

"Good God." I turned my palms up. "You left that

place less than a minute, maybe only a few seconds, before Fickler found Wallen dead!"

"I don't know." Carl wasn't fazed. "I only know I went and I didn't touch that man."

"This," I told Wolfe, "makes it even nicer. There was a slim chance we could get it that they left sooner."

"Yes." He regarded me. "It must be assumed that Wallen was alive when Ed left the booth, since that young woman—what's her name?"

"Janet."

"I call few men, and no women, by their first names. What's her name?"

"That's all I know, Janet. It won't bite you."

"Stahl," Tina said. "Janet Stahl."

"Thank you. Wallen was presumably alive when Ed left the booth, since Miss Stahl.followed him. So Miss Stahl, who saw Wallen last, and Mr. Fickler, who reported him dead—manifestly they had opportunity. What about the others?"

"You must remember," I told him, "that I had just dropped in for a shave. I had to show the right amount of intellectual curiosity but I had to be damn careful not to carry it too far. From what Ed said, I gathered that opportunity is fairly wide open, except he excludes himself. As you know, they all keep darting behind that partition for one thing or another. Ed can't remember who did and who didn't during that ten or fifteen minutes, and it's a safe bet that the others can't remember either. The fact that the cops were interested enough to ask shows that Carl and Tina haven't got a complete monopoly on it. As Ed remarked, they've gotta have evidence, and they're still looking."

Wolfe grunted in disgust.

"It also shows," I went on, "that they haven't got any real stopper to cork it, like prints from the car or localizing the scissors or anything they found on the corpse. They sure want Carl and Tina, and you know what happens when they get them, but they're still short on exhibits. If you like your suggestion to keep our guests here until Cramer and Stebbins get their paws on the right guy it might work fine as a long-term policy, but you're against the idea of women living here, or even a woman, and after a few months it might get on your nerves."

"It is no good," Tina said, back to her gasping whisper again. "Just let us go! I beg you, do that! We'll find our way to the country, we know how. You are wonderful detectives, but it is no good!"

Wolfe ignored her. He leaned back, closed his eyes, and heaved a deep sigh, and from the way his nose began to twitch I knew he was coercing himself into facing the hard fact that he would have to go to work—either that or tell me to call Purley, and that was ruled out of bounds by both his self-respect and his professional vanity. The Vardas family sat gazing at him, not in hope, but not in utter despair either. I guess they had run out of despair long ago and had none left to call on. I watched Wolfe too, his twitching nose until it stopped, and then his lips in their familiar movement, pushed out and then pulled in, out and in again, which meant he had accepted the inevitable and was getting the machinery going. I had seen him like that for an hour at a stretch, but this time it was only minutes.

He sighed again, opened his eyes, and rasped at Tina, "Except for Mr. Fickler, that man questioned you first. Is that right?"

"Yes, sir."

"Tell me what he said. What he asked. I want every word."

I thought Tina did pretty well under the circumstances. Convinced that her goose was cooked and that therefore what Wallen had asked couldn't affect her fate one way or the other, she tried to play ball anyway. She wrinkled her brow and concentrated, and it looked as if Wolfe got it all out of her. But she couldn't give him what she didn't have.

He kept after it. "You are certain he produced no object, showed you no object whatever?"

"Yes, I'm sure he didn't."

"He asked about no object, anything, in the shop?"

"No."

"He mentioned no object at all?"

"No."

"He took nothing from his pocket?"

"No."

"The newspaper he had. Didn't he take that from his pocket?"

"No, like I said, he had it in his hand when he came in the booth."

"In his hand or under his arm?"

"In his hand. I think—yes, I'm sure."

"Was it folded up?"

"Well, of course newspapers are folded."

"Yes, Mrs. Vardas. Just remember the newspaper as you saw it in his hand. I'm making a point of it because there is nothing else to make a point of, and we must have a point if we can find one. Was the newspaper folded up as if he had had it in his pocket?"

"No, it wasn't." She was trying hard. "It wasn't folded that much. Like I said, it was a *News*. When he sat down he put it on the table, at the end by his right hand—yes, that's right, my left hand; I moved some of my things to make room—and it was the way it is on the newsstand, so that's all it was folded."

"But he didn't mention it?"

"No."

"And you noticed nothing unusual about it? I mean the newspaper?"

She shook her head. "It was just a newspaper."

Wolfe repeated the performance with Carl and got more of the same. No object produced or mentioned, no hint of any. The only one on exhibit, the newspaper, had been there on the end of the table when Carl, sent by Fickler, had entered and sat, and Wallen had made no reference to it. Carl was more practical than Tina. He didn't work as hard as she had trying to remember Wallen's exact words, and I must say I couldn't blame him.

Wolfe gave up trying to get what they didn't have. He leaned back, compressed his lips, closed his eyes, and tapped with his forefingers on the ends of his chair arms. Carl and Tina looked at each other a while, then she got up and went to him, started combing his hair with her fingers, saw I was looking, began to blush, God knows why, and went back to her chair.

Finally Wolfe opened his eyes. "Confound it," he said peevishly, "it's impossible. Even if I had a move to make I couldn't make it. If I so much as stir a finger Mr. Cramer will start yelping, and I have no muzzle for him. Any effort to—"

The doorbell rang. During lunch Fritz had been told to leave it to me, so I arose, crossed to the hall, and went front. But not all the way. Four paces short of the door I saw, through the one-way glass panel, the red rugged face and the heavy broad shoulders. I wheeled and returned to the office, not dawdling, and told Wolfe, "The man to fix the chair."

"Indeed." His head jerked up. "The front room."

"I could tell him—"

"No."

Carl and Tina, warned by our tone and tempo, were on their feet. The bell rang again. I moved fast to the door to the front room and pulled it open, telling them, "In here quick. Step on it." They obeyed without a word, as if they had known me and trusted me for years, but what choice did they have? When they has passed through I said, "Relax and keep quiet," shut the door, glanced at Wolfe and got a nod, went to the hall and to the door, opened it, and said morosely, "Hello. What now?"

"It took you long enough," Inspector Cramer growled, crossing the threshold.

IV

WOLFE can move when he wants to. I have seen him prove it more than once, as he did then. By the time I was back in the office, following Cramer, he had scattered in front of him on his desk pads of paper, pencils, and a dozen folders of plant germination records for which he had had to go to the filing cabinet. One of the folders was spread open, and he was scowling at us above it. He grunted a greeting but not a welcome. Cramer grunted back, moved to the red leather chair, and planted himself in it.

I got myself at my desk. I was wishing I wasn't involved so I could just enjoy it. If Wolfe succeeded in keeping Cramer's claws off of the Vardas family and at the same time kept himself out of jail I would show my appreciation by not hitting him for a raise for at least a month.

Fritz entered with a tray, so Wolfe had found time to push a buttom too. It was the fixed allotment, three bottles of beer. Wolfe, getting the opener from his drawer, told Fritz to bring another glass, but Cramer said no thanks.

Suddenly Cramer looked at me and demanded, "Where did you go when you left the barber shop?"

My brows went up. "Just like that?"

"Yes."

"Well, then. If you really cared you could have put a tail on me. If you didn't care enough to put a tail on me you're just being nosy, and I resent it. Next question."

"Why not answer that one?"

"Because some of the errands I get sent on are confidential, and I don't want to start a bad habit."

Cramer turned abruptly to Wolfe. "You know a police officer was killed this morning there in that shop."

"Yes." Wolfe halted a foaming glass on its way to his mouth. "Archie told me about it."

"Maybe he did."

"Not maybe. He did."

"Okay." Cramer cocked his head and watched Wolfe empty the glass and use his handkerchief on his lips. Then he said, "Look. This is what brought me here. I have learned over a stretch of years that when I find you within a mile of a murder, and Goodwin is a part of you, something fancy can be expected. I don't need to itemize that; your memory is as good as mine. Wait a second, let me finish. I don't say there's no such thing as a coincidence. I know you've been going to that shop for two years, and Goodwin for six years. It wouldn't be so remarkable if he happened in there this particular day, two hours after a murder, if it wasn't for certain features. He told Graboff, his barber, that he needed an emergency shave to go to an appointment. Incidentally, it couldn't have been much of an emergency, since he waited nearly half an hour while Graboff finished with a customer, but I might concede that. The point is that Graboff and Fickler both say that in the six years Goodwin has been going there he has never gone just for a shave. Not once. He goes only for the works, haircut, scalp massage, shampoo, and shave. That makes it too remarkable. Just one day in six years an emergency sends him there for a shave, and this is the day. I don't believe it."

Wolfe shrugged. "Then you don't. I'm not responsible for your credulity quotient, Mr. Cramer. Neither is Mr. Goodwin. I don't see how we can help you."

"Nobody would believe it," Cramer said stubbornly, refusing to get riled. "That's why I'm here. I do believe that Goodwin went to that shop because he knew a man had been murdered there."

"Then you believe wrong," I told him. "Your credulity quotient needs an overhaul. Until I got there I hadn't the slightest idea or suspicion that a man had been murdered, there or anywhere else."

"You have been known to lie, Goodwin."

"Only within limits, and I know what they are. I will state that in an affidavit. Write it out, and there's a notary at the corner drugstore. That would be perjury, which I'm allergic to."

"Your going there had nothing whatever to do with the murder?"

"Put it that way if you prefer it. It did not."

Wolfe was pouring beer. "How," he inquired, not belligerently, "was Mr. Goodwin supposed to have learned of the murder? Had you fitted that in?"

"I don't know." Cramer gestured impatiently. "I didn't come here with a diagram. I only know what it means, what it always has meant, when I'm on a homicide, which is what I work at, and suddenly there you are, or Goodwin. And there Goodwin was, two hours after it happened, and I asked some questions and I can take only so much coincidence. Frankly I have no idea where you come in. You work only for big money. That hit-and-run driver could be a man with money, but if so it couldn't be someone who works in that shop. No one there has the kind of dough that hires Nero Wolfe. So I don't see how it could be money that pulled you in, and I frankly admit I have no idea what else could. I guess I'll have a little beer after all, if you don't mind. I'm tired."

Wolfe leaned forward to push the button.

"What was on my mind," Cramer said, "was two things. First, I did not believe that Goodwin just happened to drop in at the scene of a murder. I admit he's not quite brazen enough to commit perjury." He looked at me. "I want that affidavit. Today. Word it yourself, but say it right."

"You'll get it," I assured him.

"Today."

"Yep."

"Don't forget it."

Fritz entered with another tray, put it down on the little table at Cramer's elbow, and uncapped the bottle. "Shall I pour, sir?"

"Thanks, I will." Cramer took the glass in his left hand, tilted it, and poured with his right. Unlike Wolfe, he didn't care for a lot of foam. "Second," he said, "I thought that what took Goodwin there might be something you would be ready to tell me about, but he wouldn't because you're the boss and he's such a goddam clam unless you say the word. I don't pretend to have anything to pry it out of you with. You know the law about withholding evidence as well as I do, you ought to by this time, the stunts you've pulled—"

The foam was down to where he liked it, and he stopped to take a swig.

"You thought," Wolfe asked, "that I had sent Archie to the shop on business?"

Cramer ran his tongue over his lips. "Yes. For the reason given. I still think so."

"You're wrong. I didn't. Since you're to get an affidavit from Archie, you might as well have one from me too and get it settled. In it I will say that I did not send him to the barber shop, that I did not know he was going there, and that I heard and knew nothing of the murder until he returned and told me."

"You'll swear to that?"

"As a favor to you, yes. You've wasted your time coming here, and you might as well get a little something out of it." Wolfe reached for his second bottle. "By the way, I still don't know why you came. According to Archie, the murderer is known and all you have to do is find him—that man at the clothes rack—uh, Carl. And his wife, you said, Archie?"

"Yes, sir. Tina, one of the manicures. Purley told me straight they had done it and scooted."

Wolfe frowned at Cramer. "Then what could you expect to get from me? How could I help?"

"What I said, that's all," Cramer insisted doggedly, pouring the rest of his beer. "When I see Goodwin poking around I want to know why."

"I don't believe it," Wolfe said rudely. He turned to me. "Archie. I think you're responsible for this. You're brash and you talk too much. I think it was something you did or said. What was it?"

"Sure, it's always me." I was hurt. "What I did, I got a shave, and Ed had a customer and I had to wait, so I talked with Purley and looked at a magazine—no, I started to but didn't—and with Inspector Cramer and then with Janet, Miss Stahl to you, and with Ed while I was in the chair—that is, he talked—"

"What did you say to Mr. Cramer?"

"Practically nothing. Just answered a civil question."

"What did you say to Mr. Stebbins?"

I thought I knew now where he was headed and hoped to God I was right. "Oh, just asked what was going on, and he told me. I've told you about it."

"Not verbatim. What did you say?"

"Nothing, damn it! Of course Purley wanted to know what brought me there, and I told him I—say, wait a minute! Maybe you're right at that! He asked me if I had seen Carl or Tina this morning, and I said sure, I had put them here in the front room and told them to wait, and if he would step on it—"

"Ha!" Wolfe snorted. "I knew it! Your confounded tongue. So that's it." He looked at Cramer. "Why have you waited to pounce?" he asked, trying not to sound too contemptuous, for after all Cramer was drinking his beer. "Since Archie has rashly disclosed our little secret, it would be useless for me to try to keep it. That's what we use the front room for mainly, to keep murderers in. You're armed, I suppose? Go in and get them. Archie, open the door for him."

I went to the door to the front room and pulled it open, not too wide. "I'm scared of murderers myself," I said courteously, "or I'd be glad to help."

Cramer had a glass half full of beer in his hand, and it may well be that that took the trick. Bullheaded as he was, he might have been capable of getting up and walking over for a look into the room, even though our build-up had convinced him it was empty, not caring how much we would enjoy it or how silly he would look coming out. But the glass of beer complicated it. He would either have to take it with him or reach first to put it down on the little table—or throw it at Wolfe.

"Nuts," he said and lifted the glass to drink.

I swung the door to carelessly, without bothering to see that it latched, and yawned on the way back to my chair.

"At least," Wolfe said, rubbing it in, "I can't be jailed for harboring a fugitive—one of your favorite threats. But I really don't know what you're after. If it was those two you'll get them, of course. What else is there?"

"Nothing but a little more evidence." Cramer glanced at his wristwatch. "I'll get down to my office. That's where I started for, and this was on the way so I thought I'd stop to see what you had to say. We'll get 'em all right. It don't pay to kill a cop in this town." He stood up. "It wouldn't pay for anyone to hide a cop-killer in their front room, either. Thanks for the beer. I'll be expecting those affidavits, and in case—"

The phone rang. I swiveled and got it. "Nero Wolfe's office, Archie Goodwin speaking."

"Inspector Cramer there?"

I said yes, hold it. "For you," I told him and moved aside, and he came and took it. He spoke not more than twenty words altogether, between spells of listening. He dropped the phone onto the cradle, growled something about more trouble, and headed for the door.

"Have they found 'em?" I asked his back.

"No." He didn't turn. "Someone's hurt—the Stahl girl."

I marched after him, thinking the least I could do was cooperate by opening another door for him, but he was there and on out before I caught up, so I about-faced and returned to the office.

Wolfe was standing up, and I wondered why all the exertion, but a glance at the wall clock showed me 3:55, nearly time for his afternoon visit to the plant rooms.

"He said Janet got hurt," I stated.

Wolfe, finishing the last of his beer, grunted.

"I owe Janet something. Besides, it could mean that Carl and Tina are out of it. We ought to know, and they would like to know. I don't usually get shaved twice a day, but there's no law against it. I can be there in ten minutes. Why not?"

"No." He put the glass down. "We'll see."

"I don't feel like we'll seeing. I need to do something. I lost ten pounds in ten seconds, standing there holding that doorknob, trying to look as if it would be fun to watch him coming to look in. If it wasn't for our guests I almost wish he had, just to see what you would do, not to mention me. I've got to do something now."

"There's nothing to do." He looked at the clock and moved. "Put those folders back, please?" Halfway to the door he turned. "Disturb me only if it is unavoidable. And admit no more displaced persons to the house. Two at a time is enough."

"It was you who fed—" I began with feeling, but he was gone. In a moment I heard the sound of his elevator.

I put the folders away and took the beer remains to the kitchen and then went to the front room. Tina, who was lying on the couch, sat up as I entered and saw to her skirt hem. She had nice legs, but my mind was occupied.

Carl, on a chair near the foot of the couch, stood up and asked a string of questions with his eyes.

"As you were," I told them gruffly. I heartily agreed with Wolfe that two was enough. "I hope you didn't go near the windows?"

"We have learned so long ago to stay away from windows," Carl said. "But we want to go. We will pay the fifty dollars gladly."

"You can't go." I was irritated and emphatic. "That was Inspector Cramer, a very important policeman. We told him you were in here, and so—"

"You told him—" Tina gasped.

"Yes. It's the Hitler-Stalin technique in reverse. They tell barefaced lies to have them taken for the truth, and we told the barefaced truth to have it taken for a lie. It worked. You were within a hair's breadth of getting flushed, and I'll never be the same again, but it worked. So now we're stuck, and you are too. You stay here. We've told the cops you're in this room, and you're not going to leave it, at least not until bedtime. I'm locking you in." I pointed to a door. "That's a bathroom, and there's a glass if you want a drink. It has another door into the office, but I'll lock it. The windows have bars."

I crossed to the door to the hall and locked it with my master key. I went through to the office, entered the bathroom in the corner, turned the bolt flange on the door to the front room, opened the door an inch, returned to the office, locked that door with my key, and went back to the front room. Carl and Tina, speaking in low tones, fell silent as I entered.

"All set," I told them. "Make yourselves comfortable. If you need anything don't yell, this room is soundproofed; push this button." I put my finger on it, under the edge of the table. "I'll give you the news as soon as there is any." I was going.

"But this is hanging in the air on a thread," Carl protested.

"You're damn right it is," I agreed grimly. "Your only hope is that Mr. Wolfe has now put his foot in it, and it's up to him to get both you and him loose, not to mention me. He can't possibly do it, which is an advantage, because the only things he ever really strains himself on are those that can't be done. The next two hours are time out. He doesn't let anything interfere with his afternoon session, from four to six, with his orchids up on the roof. By the way, there is a small gleam. Inspector Cramer beat it back to the shop because he got a phone call that Janet had been hurt. If she got hurt with scissors with you not there, it may be a real break."

"Janet?" Tina was distressed. "Was she hurt much?"

I looked at her suspiciously. Surely that was phony. But she looked as if she really meant it. Maybe with some people who have been hurt plenty and often themselves, that's the way they react when someone else gets it, some-one they know.

"I don't know," I said, "and I'm not going to try to find out. Curiosity can be justified only up to a point, and this is no time to stretch it. We'll have to sit it out, at least until six o'clock." I glanced at my wrist. "That's only an hour and twenty minutes. Then we'll see if Mr. Wolfe has cooked up a charade. If not, he may at least invite you to dinner. See you later."

As I turned to go Carl sprang and broke my neck.

I have had enough unpleasant surprises over the years so that I am never completely off guard, but I admit I was careless that time because I underestimated him. He was a full three inches and thirty pounds under me, but I should have known that a guy who had managed a geta-way from a concentration camp, and also from a continent, must have learned some good tricks. He had. The one he tried on me took him off the floor and through the air at my back, got his knees in my spine and his arm hooked under my chin. I was careless, but not quite careless enough. I heard and felt his rush too late to wheel or step, but in time to arch my back and drop my chin. He fas-tened onto me piggyback, and his muscles were a real sur-prise.

If he was that quick on the spring he might be just as quick with his left hand getting out a knife, so I didn't try to get subtle. I bent my knees, called on my legs for all they had, jumped straight up as high as I could with him on me, jerked backwards in the air to horizontal, and hit the floor—or he did, with me on top. It squashed air out of him and jolted his arm loose. I bounced off to the right, got my feet under me, and came up, facing Tina in case she was prepared to help.

She wasn't. She was just standing there, frozen, with no blood left in her, anyway not in her face. I moved my head a little from left to right and then slowly in a circle. "I thought he broke my neck," I told her, "but he didn't. He only tried to."

She had no comment. Carl was on the floor, pulling air in for replacement. I stepped to him, reached down for his arm, yanked him upright, and went over him good. The only tool he had was a pocket knife with two little blades.

I backed up a step and remarked, "You act on impulse, don't you?"

"I couldn't break your neck," he said, as if his feelings were hurt. "You're too strong."

"You sure could try."

"No. I only wanted to go. If we stay here there is no hope. It would have made you numb, that was all."

"Yeah. Napoleon's been numb for over a century. I hope your ribs hurt. If so, think of me."

I went to the door to the office, passed through, closed the door, and locked it. There in privacy I took a survey, physical and mental. It was no pleasure to move my head, especially backward, but it did move. My back was sore where his knees had hit it, but some assorted twisting and bending proved that all the joints worked without cracking. I sat at my desk for the mental part. Getting my neck broke, or damn near it, had cleared my brain. Being smart enough to get it in that neither Carl nor Tina could drive a car was all right as far as it went, but it proved nothing at all about the scissors in Jake Wallen's back; it merely showed that there are motives and motives. The cops thought Wallen had been killed by a cornered hit-and-run driver, but what did I think? And even more important, what did Wolfe think? Was he up ahead of me as usual, or was he being too offhand, since no fee was involved, and maybe letting us in for a bloody nose?

I sat and surveyed and got so dissatisfied that I rang the plant rooms, told Wolfe about Carl's attempt to numb me, and tried to go on from there, but he brushed me off and said it could wait until six o'clock. I sat some more, practiced moving my head in various directions, and then got up to do back exercises. I was bending to touch the floor with my fingers when the phone rang.

It was Sergeant Purley Stebbins. "Archie? Purley. I'm at the barber shop. We want you here quick."

Two things told me it was no hostile mandate: his tone and the "Archie." The nature of my encounters with him usually had him calling me Goodwin, but occasionally it was Archie.

I responded in kind. "I'm busy but I guess so. If you really want me. Do you care to specify?"

"When you get here. You're needed, that's all. Grab a cab."

I buzzed Wolfe on the house phone and reported the development. Then I got a gun from the drawer, went to the kitchen and gave it to Fritz, described the status of the guests, and told him to keep his eyes and ears open. Then I hopped.

V

THE crowd of spectators ganged up in the corridor outside the Goldenrod Barber Shop was twice as big as it had been before, for two reasons. It was just past five o'clock, and home-goers were flocking through for the subway; and inside the shop there was a fine assortment of cops and dicks to look at. The corridor sported not one flatfoot, but three, keeping people away from the entrance and moving. I told one of them my name and errand and was ordered to wait, and in a minute Purley came and escorted me in.

I darted a glance around. The barber chairs were all empty. Fickler and three of the barbers, Jimmie, Ed, and Philip, were seated along the row of waiting chairs, in their white jackets, each with a dick beside him. Tom was not in view. Other city employees were scattered around.

Purley had guided me to the corner by the cash register. "How long have you known that Janet Stahl?" he demanded.

I shook my head reproachfully. "Not that way. You said I was needed, and I came on the run. If you merely want my biography, call at the office any time during hours. If you call me Archie, even after hours."

"Cut the comedy. How long have you known her?"

"No, sir. I know a lawyer. Lay a foundation."

Purley's right shoulder twitched. It was only a reflex of his impulse to sock me, beyond his control and therefore nothing to resent. "Some day," he said, setting his jaw and then releasing it. "She was found on the floor of her booth, out from a blow on her head. We brought her to, and she can talk but she won't. She won't tell us anything. She says she don't know us. She says she won't talk to anybody except her friend Archie Goodwin. How long have you known her?"

"I'm touched," I said with emotion. "Until today I've merely leered at her, with no conversation or bodily contact of any kind. The only chat I've ever had with her was here today under your eye, but look what it did to her. Is it any wonder my opinion of myself is what it is?"

"Listen, Goodwin, we're after a murderer."

"I know you are. I'm all for it."

"You've never seen her outside this shop?"

"No."

"That can be checked maybe. Right now we want you to get her to talk. Goddam her, she's stopped us dead. Come on." He moved.

I caught his elbow. "Hold it. If she sticks to it that she'll only talk with me I'll have to think up questions. I ought to know what happened."

"Yeah." Purley wanted no more delay, but obviously I had a point. "There were only three of us left, me here at

the front, and Joffe and Sullivan there on chairs. The barbers were all working on customers. Fickler was moving
around. I was on the phone half the time. We had
squeezed out everything we could here, for the present
anyhow, and it was a letdown, you know how that is."

"Where was Janet?"

"I'm telling you. Toracco, that's Philip, finished with a
customer, and a new one got in his chair—we were letting
regular customers in. The new one wanted a manicure, and
Toracco called Janet, but she didn't come. Fickler was
helping the outgoing customer on with his coat. Toracco
went behind the partition to get Janet, and there she was
on the floor of her booth, cold. She had gone there fifteen
minutes before, possibly twenty. I think all of them had
gone behind the partition at least once during that time."

"You think?"

"Yes, I think."

"It must have been quite a letdown."

"I said I was on the phone a lot. Joffe and Sullivan will
not be jumped up, and don't they know it. You know damn
well how much we like it, her getting bopped with three of
us right here."

"How bad is she hurt?"

"Not enough for the hospital. Doc let us keep her here.
She was hit above the right ear with a bottle taken from the
supply shelf against the partition, six feet from the entrance to her booth. The bottle was big and heavy, full of
oil. It was there by her on the floor."

"Prints?"

"For God's sake, start a school. He had a towel in his
hand or something. Come on."

"One second. What did the doctor say when you asked
him if she could have been just testing her skull?"

"He said it was possible but he doubted it. Come and
ask her."

Feeling that I had enough for a basis for conversation, I
followed him. As we went toward the partition all the
barbers and dicks along the row of chairs gave us looks,
none of them cheerful. Fickler was absolutely forlorn.

I had never been behind the partition before. The space

ran about half the length of the shop. Against the partition were steamers, vats, lamps, and other paraphernalia, and then a series of cupboards and shelves. Across a wide aisle were the manicure booths, four of them, though I had never seen more than two operators in the shop. As we passed the entrance to the first booth in the line a glance showed me Inspector Cramer seated at a little table across from Tom, the barber with white hair. Cramer saw me and arose. I followed Purley to the third booth, and on in. Then steps came behind me, and Cramer was there.

It was a big booth, eight by eight, but was now crowded. In addition to us three and the furniture, a city employee was standing in a corner, and, on a row of chairs lined up against the right wall, Janet Stahl was lying on her back, her head resting on a stack of towels. She had moved her eyes, but not her head, to take in us visitors. She looked beautiful.

"Here's your friend Goodwin," Purley told her, trying to sound sympathetic.

"Hello there," I said professionally. "What does this mean?"

The long home-grown lashes fluttered at me. "You," she said.

"Yep. Your friend Archie Goodwin." There was a chair there, the only one she wasn't using, and I squeezed past Purley and sat, facing her and close. "How do you feel, terrible?"

"No, I don't feel at all. I am past feeling."

I reached for her wrist, got my fingers on the spot, and looked at my watch. In thirty seconds I said, "Your pump isn't bad. May I inspect your head?"

"If you're careful."

"Groan if it hurts." I used all fingers to part the fine brown hair, and gently but thoroughly investigated the scalp. She closed her eyes and flinched once, but there was no groan. "A lump to write home about," I announced. "Doing your hair will be a problem. I'd like to give the guy that did it a piece of my mind before plugging him. Who was it?"

"Send them away, and I'll tell you."

I turned to the kibitzers. "Get out," I said sternly. "If I had been here this would never have happened. Leave us."

They went without a word. I sat listening to the sound of their retreating footsteps outside in the aisle, then thought I had better provide sound to cover in case they were careless tiptoeing back. They had their choice of posts, just outside the open entrance or in the adjoining booths. The partitions were only six feet high. "It was dastardly," I said. "He might have killed you or disfigured you for life, and either one would have ruined your career. Thank God you've got a good strong thick skull."

"I started to scream," she said, "but it was too late."

"What started you to scream? Seeing him, or hearing him?"

"It was both. I wasn't in my chair, I was in the customer's chair, with my back to the door—I was just sitting trying to think—and there was a little noise behind me, like a stealthy step, and I looked up and saw him reflected in the glass, right behind me with his arm raised, and I started to scream, but before I could get it out he struck—"

"Wait a minute." I got up and moved my chair to the outer side of the little table and sat in it. "These details are important. You were like this?"

"That's it. I was sitting thinking."

I felt that the opinion I had formed of her previously had not done her justice. The crinkly glass of the partition wall could reflect no object whatever, no matter how the light was. Her contempt for mental processes was absolutely spectacular. I moved my chair back beside her. From that angle, as she lay there flat on her back, not only was her face lovely to see, but the rest of her was good for the eyes too.

I asked, "But you saw his reflection before he struck?"

"Oh, yes."

"Did you recognize him?"

"Of course I did. That's why I wouldn't speak to them. That's why I had to see you. It was that big one with the big ears and gold tooth, the one they call Stebbins, or they call him Sergeant."

I wasn't surprised. I knew her quality now. "You mean it was him that hit you with the bottle?"

"I can't say it was him that hit me. I think people should be careful what they accuse other people of. I only know it was him I saw standing behind me with his arm raised, and then something hit me. From that anyone can only draw conclusions, but there are other reasons too. He was rude to me this morning, asking me questions, and all day he has been looking at me in a rude way, not the way a girl is willing for a man to look at her because she has to expect that. And then you can just be logical. Would Ed want to kill me, or Philip or Jimmie or Tom or Mr. Fickler? Why would they? So it must have been him even if I hadn't seen him."

"It does sound logical," I conceded. "But I've known Stebbins for years and have never known him to strike a woman without cause. What did he have against you?"

"I don't know." She frowned a little. "When they ask me that I'll just have to say I don't know. That's one of the first things you must tell me, how to answer things to the reporters. I shouldn't think I can keep on saying I don't know, or why would they print it? What hit you I don't know, who hit you I don't know, why did he hit you I don't know, my Lord, who would want to read that? What shall I say when they ask why he hit me?"

"We'll come back to that. First we—"

"We ought to settle it now." She was pouting fit for a *Life* cover, but determined. "That's how you'll earn your ten per cent."

"My ten per cent of what?"

"Of everything I get. As my manager." She extended a hand, her eyes straight at mine. "Shake on it."

To avoid a contractual shake without offending, I grasped the back of her hand with my left, turning her palm up, and ran the fingers of my right from her wrist to her fingertips. "It's a darned good idea," I said appreciatively, "but we'll have to postpone it. I'm going through bankruptcy just now, and it would be illegal for me to make a contract. About—"

"I can tell the reporters to ask you about things I don't know. It's called referring them to my manager."

"I know it is. Later on it will—"

"I don't need you later on. I need you right now."

"Here I am, you've got me, but not under contract yet." I released her hand, which I had kept as something to hold onto, and got emphatic. "If you tell reporters I'm your manager I'll give you a lump that will make that one seem as flat as a pool table. If they ask why he hit you don't say you don't know, say it's a mystery. People love a mystery. Now—"

"That's it!" She was delighted. "That's the kind of thing!"

"Sure. Tell 'em that. Now we've got to consider the cops. Stebbins is a cop, and they won't want it hung on him. They've had one cop killed here today already. They'll try to tie this up with that. I know how they work, I know them only too well. They'll try to make it that somebody here killed Wallen, and he found out that you knew something about it so he tried to kill you. They may even think they have some kind of evidence—for instance, something you were heard to say. So we have to be prepared. We have to go back over it. Are you listening?"

"Certainly. What do I say when the reporters ask me if I'm going to go on working here? Couldn't I say I don't want to desert Mr. Fickler in a time of trouble?"

It took control to stay in that chair. I would have given a good deal to be able to get up and walk out, go to Purley and Cramer at their eavesdropping posts, tell them she was all theirs and they were welcome to her, and go on home. But at home there were the guests locked in the front room, and sometime, somehow, we had to get rid of them. I looked at her charming enchanting comely face, with its nice chin and straight little nose and the eyelashes, and realized that the matter would be approached from her angle or not at all.

"That's the ticket," I said warmly. "Say you've got to be loyal to Mr. Fickler. That's the main thing to work on, how to handle the reporters. Have you ever been interviewed before?"

"No, this will be the first, and I want to start right."

"Good for you. What they like best of all is to get the jump on the police. If you can tell them something the cops don't know they'll love you forever. For instance, the fact that Stebbins crowned you doesn't prove that he's the only one involved. He must have an accomplice here in the shop, or why did Wallen come here in the first place? We'll call the accomplice X. Now listen. Sometime today, some time or other after Wallen's body was found, you saw something or heard something, and X knew you did. He knew it, and he knew that if you told about it—if you told me, for example—it would put him and Stebbins on the spot. Naturally both of them would want to kill you. It could have been X that tried to, but since you say you saw Stebbins reflected in the glass we'll let it go at that for now. Here's the point: if you can remember what it was you saw or heard that scared X, and if you tell the reporters before the cops get wise to it, they'll be your friends for life. Now for God's sake don't miss this chance. Concentrate. Remember everything you saw and heard here today, and everything you did and said too. Even if it takes us all night we've got to work it out."

She was frowning. "I don't remember anything that would scare anybody."

"Don't go at it like that. It was probably some little thing that didn't seem important to you at all. We may have to start at the beginning and go over every—"

I stopped on account of her face. The frown had left it, and she was looking past me, not seeing me, with an expression that told me plainly, if I knew her half as well as I thought I did, what was going on inside. I snapped at her, "Do you want the reporters hating you? Off of you for good?"

She was startled. "Of course not! That would be awful!"

"Then watch your step. This has got to be all wool. A girl with a fine mind like you, so much imaginaton, it would be a cinch for you to be creative, but don't. They'll double-check everything you say, and if they find it's not completely straight you're ruined. They'll never forgive you. You'll never need a manager."

"But I can't remember anything like that!"

"Not right off the bat, who could? Sometimes a thing like this takes days, let alone hours." Her hand was right there, and I patted it. "I guess we'd better go over it together, right straight through. That's the way Nero Wolfe would do it. What time did you get to work this morning?"

"When I always do, a quarter to nine. I'm punctual."

"Were the others already here?"

"Some were and some weren't."

"Who was and who wasn't?"

"My Lord, I don't know. I didn't notice." She was resentful. "If you're going to expect me to remember things like that we might as well quit, and you wouldn't be a good manager. When I came to work I was thinking of something else. A lot of the time I am thinking of something else, so how would I notice?"

I had to be patient. "Okay, we'll start at another point. You remember when Wallen came in and spoke with Fickler and went to Tina's booth and talked with her, and when Tina came out Fickler sent Philip in to him. You remember that?"

She nodded. "I guess so."

"Guesses won't get us anywhere. Just recall the situation, where you all were when Philip came back after talking with Wallen. Where were you?"

"I didn't notice."

"I'm not saying you noticed, but look back. There's Philip, coming around the end of the partition after talking with Wallen. Did you hear him say anything? Did you say anything to him?"

"I don't think Philip was this X," she declared. "He is married, with children. I think it was Jimmie Kirk. He tried to make passes at me when I first came, and he drinks, you can ask Ed about that, and he thinks he's superior. A barber being superior!" She looked pleased. "That's a good idea about Jimmie being X, because I don't have to say he really tried to kill me. I'll try to remember something he said. Would it matter exactly when he said it?"

I had had enough, but a man can't hit a woman when she's down, so I ended it without violence.

"Not at all," I told her, "but I've got an idea. I'll go and see if I can get something out of Jimmie. Meanwhile I'll send a reporter in to break the ice with you, from the *Gazette* probably. I know a lot of them." I was on my feet. "Just use your common sense and stick to facts. See you later."

"But Mr. Goodwin! I want—"

I was gone. Three steps got me out of the booth, and I strode down the aisle and around the end of the partition. There I halted, and it wasn't long before I was joined by Cramer and Purley. Their faces were expressive. I didn't have to ask if they had got it all.

"If you shoot her," I suggested, "send her brain to Johns Hopkins, if you can find it."

"Jesus," Purley said. That was all he said.

Cramer grunted. "Did she do it herself?"

"I doubt it. It was a pretty solid blow to raise that lump, and you didn't find her prints on the bottle. Bothering about prints is beneath her. I had to come up for air, but I left you an in. Better pick a strong character to play the role of reporter from the *Gazette*."

"Send for Biatti," Cramer snapped at Purley.

"Yeah," I agreed, "he can take it. Now I go home?"

"No. She might insist on seeing her manager again."

"I wouldn't pass that around," I warned them. "How would you like a broadcast of her line on Sergeant Stebbins? I'd like to be home for dinner. We're having fresh pork tenderloin."

"We would all like to be home for dinner." Cramer's look and tone were both sour. They didn't change when he shifted to Purley. "What about it? Is the Vardas pair still all you want?"

"They're what I want most," Purley said doggedly, "in spite of her getting it when they weren't here, but I guess we've got to spread out more. You can finish with them here and go home to dinner, and I suppose we've got to take 'em all downtown. I'm not sold that the Stahl girl is unfurnished inside her head, and we know she's capable of using her hands, since only three months ago she pushed a full-grown man out of his own car into a ditch and drove off. No matter how hard he was playing her, that's quite a stunt. I still want to be shown she couldn't have used that bottle on herself and I don't have to be shown that she could have used the scissors on Wallen if she felt like it. Or if she performed with the bottle to have something to tell reporters about, the Vardases are still what I want most. But I admit the other if is the biggest one. If some one here conked her, finding out who and why comes first until we get the Vardases."

Cramer stayed sour. "You haven't even started."

"Maybe that's a little too strong, Inspector."

"I don't think so."

"We were on the Vardases, but we didn't clear out of here, we kept close. Then when we found the Stahl girl and brought her to she shut the valve and had to see Goodwin. Even so, I wouldn't say we haven't made a start with the others. Ed Graboff plays the horses and owes a bookie nine hundred dollars, and he had to sell his car. Philip Toracco went off the rails in 1945 and spent a year in a booby hatch. Joel Fickler has been seen in public places with Horny Gallagher, and while that don't prove—"

Cramer cut in to shoot at me, "Is Fickler a racket boy?"

I shook my head. "Sorry. Blank. I've never been anything but a customer."

"If he is we'll get it." Purley was riled and didn't care who knew it. "Jimmie Kirk apparently only goes back three years, and he has expensive habits for a barber. Tom Yerkes did a turn in nineteen thirty-nine for assault, beat up a guy who took his young granddaughter for a fast weekend, and he is known for having a quick take-off. So I don't think you can say we haven't even started. We've got to take 'em all downtown and get through, especially about last night, sure we do. But I still want the Vardases."

"Are all alibis for last night being checked?" Cramer demanded.

"They have been."

"Do them over, and good. Get it going. Use as many men as you need. And not only alibis, records too. I want the Vardas pair as much as you do, but if the Stahl girl didn't use that bottle on herself, I also want someone else. Get Biatti here. Let him have a try at her before you take her down."

"He's not on duty, Inspector."

"Tell them to find him. Get him here."

"Yes, sir."

Purley moved. He went to the phone at the cashier's counter. I went to the one in the booth at the end of the clothes rack and dialed the number I knew best. Fritz answered, and I asked him to buzz the extension in the plant rooms, since it was still a few minutes short of six o'clock.

"Where are you?" Wolfe demanded. He was always testy when interrupted up there.

"At the barber shop." I was none too genial myself. "Janet was sitting in her booth and got hit on the head with a bottle of oil. They have gone through the routine and are still at the starting line. Her condition is no more critical than it was before she got hit. She insisted on seeing me, and I have had a long intimate talk with her. I can't say I made no progress, because she asked me to be her manager, and I am now giving you notice, quitting at the end of this week. Aside from that I got nowhere. She's one in a million. I would love to see you take her on. I have been requested to stick around. I'm willing, but I advise you to tell Fritz to increase the grocery orders until further notice."

Silence. Then, "Who is there?"

"Everybody. Cramer, Purley, squad men, the staff. They quit letting customers in after Janet got rapped. The whole party will be moved downtown in an hour or so, including Janet. Everyone is glum, including me."

"No progress whatever has been made?"

"Not as far as I know, except what I told you, I am now Janet's manag—"

"Pfui." Silence. In a moment, "Stay there."

The connection went.

I left the booth. Neither Purley nor Cramer was in sight. Only one flatfoot was at the door, and the throng outside in the corridor was no longer a throng, merely a knot, and

a small one. I moseyed toward the rear, with the line of
empty barber chairs on my left and the row of waiting
chairs against the partition on my right. Fickler was there,
and three of the barbers—Ed being the missing one now
—with dicks in between. They weren't interested in me at
all, and I made no effort to try to change their attitude.

The chair on the left of the magazine table was empty,
and I dropped into it. Apparently no one had felt like
reading today, since the same *New Yorker* was on top and
the two-weeks-old *Time* was still on the shelf below. I
would have been glad to employ my mind analyzing the
situation if there had been anything to analyze, but there
was no place to start, and after sitting a few minutes I became aware that I was trying to analyze Janet. Of course
that was even more hopeless, and I mention it only to
show you the condition I was in. But it did look as if Janet
was the key, and in that case the thing to do was to figure
some way of handling her. I sat and worked on that problem. There must be some practical method of digging up
from her memory the fact or facts that we had to have.
Hypnotize her, maybe? That might work. I was considering
suggesting it to Cramer when I became aware of movement over at the door and lifted my eyes.

The flatfoot was blocking the entrance to keep a man
fully twice his weight from entering, and was explaining
the situation.

The man let him finish and then spoke. "I know, I
know." His eyes came at me over the flatfoot's shoulder,
and he bellowed, "Archie! Where's Mr. Cramer?"

VI

I GOT up and made for the door in no haste or jubilation.
There have been times when the sight and sound of
Wolfe have given me a lift, but that wasn't one of them. I
had told him on the phone that I would love to see him
take Janet on, but that had been rhetorical. One would
get him ten he couldn't make a dent in her.

"Do you want in?" I asked.

"What the devil," he roared, "do you suppose I came for?"

"Okay, take it easy. I'll go see—"

But I didn't have to go. His first bellow had carried within, and Cramer's voice came from right behind me. "Well! Dynamite?"

"I'll be damned," Purley, there too, growled.

The flatfoot had moved aside, leaving it to the brass, and Wolfe had crossed the sill. "I came to get a haircut," he stated and marched past the sergeant and inspector to the rack, took off his hat, coat, vest, and tie, hung them up, crossed to Jimmie's chair, the second in the line, and got his bulk up onto the seat. In the mirrored wall fronting him he had a panorama of the row of barbers and dicks in his rear, and without turning his head he called, "Jimmie! If you please?"

Jimmie's dancing dark eyes came to Cramer and Purley, there by me. So did others. Cramer stood scowling at Wolfe. We all held our poses while Cramer slowly lifted his right hand and carefully and thoroughly scratched the side of his nose with his forefinger. That attended to, he decided to sit down. He went, not in a hurry, to the first chair in the line, the one Fickler himself used occasionally when there was a rush, turned it to face Wolfe, and mounted. He spoke.

"You want a haircut, huh?"

"Yes, sir. As you can see, I need one."

"Yeah." Cramer turned his head. "All right, Kirk. Come and cut his hair."

Jimmie got up and went past the chair to the cabinet for an apron. Everybody stirred, as if a climax had been reached and passed. Purley strode to the third chair in the line, Philip's, and got on it. That way he and Cramer had Wolfe surrounded, and it seemed only fair for me to be handy, so I detoured around Cramer, pulled Jimmie's stool to one side, and perched on it.

Jimmie had Wolfe aproned, and his scissors were singing above the right ear. Wolfe barred clippers.

"You just dropped in," Cramer rasped. "Like Goodwin this morning."

"Certainly not." Wolfe was curt but not pugnacious. There was no meeting of eyes, since Cramer had Wolfe's profile straight and Wolfe had Cramer's profile in the mirror. "You summoned Mr. Goodwin. He told me on the phone of his fruitless talk with Miss Stahl, and I thought it well to come."

Cramer grunted. "Okay, you're here. You won't leave your place on business for anybody or any fee, but you're here. And you're not going to leave until I know why, without any such crap as murderers in your front room."

"Not as short behind as last time," Wolfe commanded.

"Yes, sir." Jimmie had never had as big or attentive an audience and he was giving a good show. The comb and scissors flitted and sang.

"Naturally," Wolfe said tolerantly, "I expected that. You can badger me if that's what you're after, and get nowhere, but I offer a suggestion. Why not work first? Why don't we see if we can settle this business, and then, if you still insist, go after me? Or would you rather harass me than catch a murderer?"

"I'm working now. I want the murderer. What about you?"

"Forget me for the moment. You can hound me any time. I would like to propose certain assumptions about what happened here today. Do you care to hear them?"

"I'll listen, but don't drag it out."

"I won't. Please don't waste time challenging the assumptions; I don't intend to defend them, much less validate them. They are merely a basis of exploration, to be tested. The first is this, that Wallen found something in the car, the car that had killed two women—no, I don't like it this way. I want a direct view, not reflections. Jimmie, turn me around, please."

Jimmie whirled the chair a half-turn, so that Wolfe's back was to the mirrored wall, also to me, and he was facing those seated in the chairs against the partition, with Cramer on his right and Purley on his left.

"That right, sir?"

"Yes. Thank you."

I spoke up. "Ed isn't here."

"I left him in the booth," Purley rumbled.

"Get him," Wolfe instructed. "And Miss Stahl, where is she?"

"In her booth, lying down. With her head."

"We want her. She can sit up, can't she?"

"I don't know. God only knows."

"Archie. Bring Miss Stahl."

He had a nerve picking on me, with an inspector and a sergeant and three dicks there, but I postponed telling him so and went, as Purley went for Ed. In the booth Janet was still on her back on the chairs, her eyes wide open. At sight of me she fired immediately.

"You said you were going to send a reporter, but I've been thinking—"

I raised my voice to top her. "Listen to me, girlie. You're getting a break. Nero Wolfe is here with a suggestion and wants your opinion of it. Can you sit up a while?"

"Certainly I can, but—"

"No buts. He's waiting for you. Shall I carry you?"

"Certainly not!" She started up.

"Take it easy." I put an arm behind her shoulders and got her upright and then onto her feet. "Are you dizzy?"

"I'm never dizzy," she said scornfully and moved. I kept hold of her arm. She was a little unsteady on the way down the aisle to the end of the partition, but when we came in view of the audience she shook me off and went on solo. She wasn't taking help from a man, and of course I wasn't her manager yet. She took the chair I had vacated when Wolfe appeared, next to the magazine table. Ed had been brought by Purley, who was back in Philip's chair, flanking Wolfe. I returned to the stool.

Jimmie-had finished above the ears and was doing the back, so Wolfe's head was tilted forward.

"Your assumptions?" Cramer asked impatiently.

"Yes. I was saying, the first is that Wallen found something in the car that led him to this shop. It couldn't have been something he was told, for there was no one to tell him anything. It was some object. I asked you not to challenge me, but I didn't mean to exclude contradictions. If there are facts that repudiate this assumption, or any other, I want them by all means."

"We made that one without any help."

"And it still holds?"

"Yes."

"Good. That's fortunate, since all of my assumptions concern that object. The second is that Wallen had it with him when he came here. I can support that with sound—"

"You don't need to. We made it and we hold it."

"Very well. That saves time. Not too short back there, Jimmie."

"No, sir."

"The third is that he had the object inside the newspaper he was carrying. This is slenderer, but it must be tested. He had not bought the paper shortly before coming here, for it was an early edition of the *News*, on sale last evening, not on sale this morning. It was not merely stuffed in his pocket, not merely not discarded; he had it in his hand, not folded up, as it is stacked on the newsstand. It is—"

"You know a lot about it," Cramer growled.

"Do me later," Wolfe snapped. "I know nothing you don't know. It is difficult to account for his carrying a stale newspaper in that manner except on the assumption that it was a container for some object—at least, the assumption is good enough to work on. The fourth is that, whatever the object was, the murderer got it and disposed of it. More than an assumption, that is. No object that could have led him to this shop was found on Wallen's person or in the booth, so if he had it the murderer got it. The fifth assumption is that the murderer was neither Carl nor Tina. I shall—"

"What the hell!" Purley blurted.

"Ah," Cramer said. "Tell us why."

"No. I shall not support that assumption; I merely make it and submit it to our test. Don't waste time clawing at me. Since Carl and Tina are not involved and therefore didn't take the object away with them, it is still here in the shop. That is the sixth assumption, and it is good only if your surveillance of these people here all these hours has been constant and alert. What about it? Could any of them have removed such an object from the shop?"

"I want to know," Cramer demanded, "why you're excluding Carl and Tina."

"No. Not now." Wolfe and Cramer couldn't see each other because Jimmie was in between, starting on the top. "First we'll complete this test. We must know whether the object has been removed, *not* by Carl or Tina."

"No," Purley said.

"How good a no?"

"Good enough for me. No man has stepped outside this shop alone. Something could have been slipped to a customer, but that's stretching it, and we've had them under our eyes."

"Not, apparently, the one who assaulted Miss Stahl."

"That was in the shop. Is that a point?"

"I suppose not. Then we assume that the object is still here. The seventh and last assumption is this, that no proper search for such an object has been made. I hasten to add, Mr. Stebbins, that that is not a point either. You and your men are unquestionably capable of making a proper search, but I assume that you haven't done so here on account of Carl and Tina. Thinking them guilty, naturally you thought they wouldn't leave an incriminating object behind them. However, I can just ask you. Have you searched thoroughly?"

"We've looked."

"Yes. But granting all my assumptions, which of course you don't, has there been a proper search?"

"No."

"Then it's about time. Mr. Fickler!"

Fickler nearly jumped out of his skin. He, like all the others, had been buried, intent on Wolfe's buildup, and the sudden pop and crackle of his own name startled him. He jerked his head up, and I had never seen his pudgy face look so bloated.

"Me?" he squeaked.

"You run this place and can help us. However, I address all of you who work here. Put your minds on this. You too, Jimmie. Stop a moment and listen."

"I can work and listen too."

"No. I want full attention."

Jimmie backed off a step and stood.

"This," Wolfe said, "could take a few minutes or it could take all night. What we're after is an object with something on it that identifies it as coming from this shop. Ideally it should be the name and address or phone number, but we'll take less if we have to. Since we're proceeding on my assumptions, we are supposing that it was inside the newspaper as Wallen was carrying it, so it is not a business card or match folder or bottle or comb or brush. It should be flat and of considerable dimensions. Another point, it should be easily recognizable. All of you went to the booth and were questioned by Wallen, but he showed you no such object and mentioned none. Is that correct?"

They nodded and mumbled affirmatives. Ed said "Yes!" in a loud voice.

"Then only the murderer saw it or was told of it. Wallen must for some reason have shown it to him or asked him about it, and not the rest of you; or its edge may have been protruding from the newspaper, unnoticed by the others; or the murderer may merely have suspected that Wallen had it. In any case, when opportunity offered later for him to dive into the booth and kill Wallen he got the object and disposed of it. If Mr. Stebbins is right about the surveillance that has been maintained, it is still here in the shop. I put it to you, and especially to you, Mr. Fickler: what is it and where is it?"

They looked at one another and back at Wolfe. Philip said in his thin tenor, "Maybe it was the newspaper itself."

"Possibly. I doubt it. Where is it, Mr. Cramer?"

"At the laboratory. There's nothing on it or in it that could have brought Wallen here."

"What else has been taken from here to the laboratory?"

"Nothing but the scissors and the bottle that was used on Miss Stahl."

"Then it's here. All right, Jimmie, finish."

Jimmie moved to the left of him and carried on.

"It looks to me," Purley objected in his bass rumble, "like a turkey. Even with your assumptions. Say we find something like what you want, how do we know it's it? Even if we think it's it, where does that get us?"

"We'll see when we find it." Wolfe was curt. "For one thing, fingerprints."

"Nuts. If it belongs here of course it will have their prints."

"Not *their* prints, Mr. Stebbins. Wallen's prints. If he picked it up in the car he touched it. If he touched it he left prints. As I understand it, he didn't go around touching things here. He entered, spoke to Mr. Fickler, was taken to the booth, and never left it alive. If we find anything with his prints on it we've got it. Have you equipment here? If not, I advise you to send for it at once, and also for Wallen's prints from your file. Will you do that?"

Purley grunted. He didn't move.

"Go ahead," Cramer told him. "Phone. Give him what he wants. Get it over. Then he'll give us what we want, what he's here for, or else."

Purley descended from the chair and headed for the phone at the cashier's counter.

"The search," Wolfe said, "must be thorough and will take time. First I ask all of you to search your minds. What object is here, belongs here, that meets the specifications as I have described them? Surely you can tell us. Mr. Fickler?"

"I've been thinking." Fickler shook his head. "I've been thinking hard. I don't know unless it's a towel, and why would he carry a towel like that?"

"He wouldn't. Anyway a towel wouldn't help us any, so I reject it. Philip?"

"No, sir. I don't know what."

"Tom?"

Tom just shook his head gloomily.

"Ed?"

"You've got me. Pass."

"Miss Stahl?"

"I think he might have been keeping the paper because

there was something in it he wanted to read. I know I often do that, say it's in an evening paper and I don't have time—"

"Yes. We'll consider that. Jimmie?"

"I don't know a thing like that in the shop, Mr. Wolfe. Not a thing."

"Pfui." Wolfe was disgusted. "Either you have no brains at all, or they're temporarily paralyzed, or you're all in a conspiracy. I'm looking straight at such an object right now."

From behind I couldn't see where his gaze was directed, but I didn't have to. The others could, and I saw them. Eleven pairs of eyes, including Purley's—he had finished at the phone and rejoined us—were aimed at the magazine table next to Janet's chair from eleven different angles. Up to that moment my brain may have been as paralyzed as the others', but it could still react to a stimulus. I left the stool and stood right behind Wolfe, ready if and when needed.

"You mean the magazines?" Cramer demanded.

"Yes. You suscribe to them, Mr. Fickler? They come through the mail? Then the name and address is on them."

"Not on this one," said the dick on the other side of the magazine table, picking up the *New Yorker* on top.

"Drop it!" Cramer barked. "Don't touch it!"

"No," Wolfe conceded, "that comes in a wrapper. But others don't. For instance that *Time*, there on the shelf below—the addressee is on the cover. Surely it deserves examination, and others too. What if he took it from here and had it in his pocket when he stole the car and drove up Broadway? And in the excitement of his misadventure he failed to notice that it had dropped from his pocket and was on the seat of the car? And Wallen found it there, took it, and saw the name and address on it? You have sent for the equipment and Wallen's prints, Mr. Stebbins? Then we—"

"Oh! I remember!" Janet cried. She was pointing a finger. "You remember, Jimmie? This morning I was standing here, and you came by with a hot towel and you had that magazine and you tossed it under there, and I asked if you had been steaming it, and you said—"

Jimmie leaped. I thought his prey was Janet and in spite of everything I was willing to save her life, but Wolfe and the chair were in my way and cost me a fifth of a second. And it wasn't Janet he was after, it was the magazine. He went for it in a hurtling dive and got his hands on it, but then the three dicks, not to mention Cramer and Purley, were on his neck and various other parts of him. It was a handsome pile-up. Janet, except for pulling her feet back under her chair out of harm's way, did not move, nor did she make a sound. I suppose she was considering what to say to the reporters.

"Confound it," Wolfe grumbled savagely behind me. "My barber."

Anyhow that haircut was practically done.

VII

A S STUBBORN as Cramer was, he never did learn why Wolfe went to get a haircut that day. Eventually he stopped trying.

He learned plenty about Jimmie Kirk. Kirk was wanted as a bail-jumper, under another name, in Wheeling, West Virginia, on an old charge as a car stealer, with various fancy complications such as slugging a respected citizen who had surprised him in the act. Apparently he had gone straight in New York for a couple of years and had then resumed his former avocation. Unquestionably he had been fortified with liquids that Monday evening. Driving a stolen car while drunk is a risky operation, especially with a stolen magazine in your pocket.

As for Carl and Tina, I took a strong position on them Tuesday evening in the office after they had been sent up to the south room to bed.

"You know damn well what will happen," I told Wolfe. "They won't go to Ohio or anywhere else, they'll stay here.

Some day, maybe next week, maybe next year, they'll be
confronted and they'll be in trouble. Being in trouble,
they will come to me, because Carl likes me and because I
rescued them this time—"

Wolfe snorted. "You did!"

"Yes, sir. I had already noticed that magazine there
several times, and it just happened to catch your eye.
Anyhow, I am secretly infatuated with Tina so I'll try to
help them and will get my finger caught, and you'll have
to butt in again because you can't get along without me.
It will go on like that year after year. Why not take care
of it now and live in peace? There are people in Wash-
ington who owe you something, for instance Carpenter.
Start him working on it. Do you want them hanging in
the air on a thread over your head the rest of your life?
I don't. It will cost a measly buck for a phone call, and I
can get that from the fifty they have earmarked for us.
I have Carpenter's home number, and I might as well get
him right now."

No comment.

I put my hand on the phone. "Person to person, huh?"

Wolfe grunted. "I got my naturalization papers twenty-
four years ago."

"I wasn't discussing you. You've caught it from Janet,"
I said coldly and lifted the phone and dialed.

THE SQUIRT AND
THE MONKEY

I

I was doing two things at once. With my hands I was getting my armpit holster and the Marley .32 from a drawer of my desk, and with my tongue I was giving Nero Wolfe a lecture on economics.

"The most you can hope to soak him," I stated, "is five hundred bucks. Deduct a C for twenty per cent for overhead and another C for expenses incurred, that leaves three hundred. Eighty-five per cent for income tax will leave you with forty-five bucks clear for the wear and tear on your brain and my legs, not to mention the risk. That wouldn't buy—"

"Risk of what?" He muttered that only to be courteous, to show that he had heard what I said, though actually he wasn't listening. Seated behind his desk, he was scowling, not at me but at the crossword puzzle in the London *Times*.

"Complications," I said darkly. "You heard him explain it. Playing games with a gun is sappy." I was contorted, buckling the strap of the holster. That done, I picked up my coat. "Since you're listed in the red book as a detective, and since I draw pay, such as it is, as your licensed assistant, I'm all for detecting for people on request. But this bozo wants to do it himself, using our firearm as a prop." I felt my tie to see if it was straight. I didn't cross to the large mirror on the far wall of the office for a look, because whenever I did so in Wolfe's presence he snorted. "We might just as well," I declared, "send it up to him by messenger."

"Pfui," Wolfe muttered. "It is a thoroughly conventional proceeding. You are merely out of humor because you don't like Dazzle Dan. If it were Pleistocene Polly you would be zealous."

"Nuts. I look at the comics occasionally just to be cultured. It wouldn't hurt any if you did."

I went to the hall for my things, let myself out, descended the stoop, and headed toward Tenth Avenue for a taxi. A cold gusty wind came at my back from across the Hudson, and I made it brisk, swinging my arms, to get my blood going.

It was true that I did not care for Dazzle Dan, the hero of the comic strip that was syndicated to two thousand newspapers—or was it two million?—throughout the land. Also I did not care for his creator, Harry Koven, who had called at the office Saturday evening, forty hours ago. He had kept chewing his upper lip with jagged yellow teeth, and it had seemed to me that he might at least have chewed the lower lip instead of the upper, which doesn't show teeth. Moreover, I had not cared for his job as he outlined it. Not that I was getting snooty about the renown of Nero Wolfe—a guy who has had a gun lifted has got as much right to buy good detective work as a rich duchess accused of murder—but the way this Harry Koven had programmed it he was going to do the detecting himself, so the only difference between me and a messenger boy was that I was taking a taxi instead of the subway.

Anyhow Wolfe had taken the job and there I was. I pulled a slip of paper from my pocket, typed on by me from notes taken of the talk with Harry Koven, and gave it a look.

MARCELLE KOVEN, wife
ADRIAN GETZ, friend or camp follower, maybe both
PATRICIA LOWELL, agent (manager?), promoter
PETE JORDAN, artist, draws Dazzle Dan
BYRAM HILDEBRAND, artist, also draws D.D.

One of those five, according to Harry Koven, had stolen his gun, a Marley .32, and he wanted to know which one. As he had told it, that was all there was to it, but it was a cinch that if the missing object had been an electric shaver or a pair of cufflinks it would not have called for all that lip-chewing, not to mention other signs of strain. He had gone out of his way, not once but twice, to declare that he had no reason to suspect any of the five of wanting to do any shooting. The second time he had made it so emphatic that Wolfe had grunted and I had lifted a brow.

Since a Marley .32 is by no means a collector's item, it was no great coincidence that there was one in our arsenal and that therefore we were equipped to furnish Koven with the prop he wanted for his performance. As for the performance itself, the judicious thing to do was wait and see, but there was no point in being judicious about something I didn't like, so I had already checked it off as a dud.

I dismissed the taxi at the address on Seventy-sixth Street, east of Lexington Avenue. The house had had its front done over for the current century, unlike Nero Wolfe's old brownstone on West Thirty-fifth Street, which still sported the same front stoop it had started with. To enter this one you went down four steps instead of up seven, and I did so, after noting the pink shutters at the windows of all four floors and the tubs of evergreens flanking the entrance.

I was let in by a maid in uniform, with a pug nose and lipstick about as thick as Wolfe spreads Camembert on a wafer. I told her I had an appointment with Mr. Koven. She said Mr. Koven was not yet available and seemed to think that settled it, making me no offer for my hat and coat.

I said, "Our old brownstone, run by men only, is run better. When Fritz or I admit someone with an appointment we take his things."

"What's your name?" she demanded in a tone indicating that she doubted if I had one.

A loud male voice came from somewhere within. "Is that the man from Furnari's?"

A loud female voice came from up above. "Cora, is that my dress?"

I called out, "It's Archie Goodwin, expected by Mr. Koven at noon! It is now two minutes past twelve!"

That got action. The female voice, not quite so loud, told me to come up. The maid, looking frustrated, beat it. I took off my coat and put it on a chair, and my hat. A man came through a doorway at the rear of the hall and approached, speaking.

"More noise. Noisiest goddam place. Up this way." He started up the stairs. "When you have an appointment with Sir Harry, always add an hour."

I followed him. At the top of the flight there was a large square hall with wide archways to rooms at right and left. He led me through the one at the left.

There are few rooms I can't take in at a glance, but that was one of them. Two huge TV cabinets, a monkey in a cage in a corner, chairs of all sizes and colors, rugs overlapping, a fireplace blazing away, the temperature around eighty—I gave it up and focused on the inhabitant. That was not only simpler but pleasanter. She was smaller than I would specify by choice, but otherwise acceptable, especially the wide smooth brow above the serious gray eyes, and the cheekbones. She must have been part salamander, to look so cool and silky in that oven.

"Dearest Pete," she said, "you are going to stop calling my husband Sir Harry."

I admired that as a time-saver. Instead of the usual pronouncement of names, she let me know that she was Marcelle, Mrs. Harry Koven, and that the young man was Pete Jordan, and at the same time told him something.

Pete Jordan walked across to her as for a purpose. He might have been going to take her in his arms or slap her or anything in between. But a pace short of her he stopped.

"You're wrong," he told her in his aggressive baritone. "It's according to plan. It's the only way I can prove I'm not a louse. No one but a louse would stick at this, doing this crap month after month, and here look at me just because I like to eat. I haven't got the guts to quit and starve a while, so I call him Sir Harry to make you sore, working myself up to calling him something that will make him sore, and eventually I'll come to a boil and figure out a way to make Getz sore, and then I'll get bounced and I can start starving and be an artist. It's a plan."

He turned and glared at me. "I'm more apt to go through with it if I announce it in front of a witness. You're the witness. My name's Jordan, Pete Jordan."

He shouldn't have tried glaring because he wasn't built for it. He wasn't much bigger than Mrs. Koven, and he had narrow shoulders and broad hips. An aggressive baritone and a defiant glare coming from that make-up just couldn't have the effect he was after. He needed coaching.

"You have already made me sore," she told his back in a nice low voice, but not a weak one. "You act like a brat and you're too old to be a brat. Why not grow up?"

He wheeled and snapped at her, "I look on you as a mother!"

That was a foul. They were both younger than me, and she couldn't have had more than three or four years on him.

I spoke. "Excuse me," I said, "but I am not a professional witness. I came to see Mr. Koven at his request. Shall I go hunt for him?"

A thin squeak came from behind me. "Good morning, Mrs. Koven. Am I early?"

As she answered I turned for a look at the owner of the squeak, who was advancing from the archway. He should have traded voices with Pete Jordan. He had both the size and presence for a deep baritone, with a well-made head topped by a healthy mat of gray hair nearly white. Everything about him was impressive and masterful, including the way he carried himself, but the squeak spoiled it completely. It continued as he joined us.

"I heard Mr. Goodwin, and Pete left, so I thought—"

Mrs. Koven and Pete were both talking too, and it didn't seem worth the effort to sort it out, especially when the monkey decided to join in and started chattering. Also I could feel sweat coming on my forehead and neck, overdressed as I was with a coat and vest, since Pete and the newcomer were in shirt sleeves. I couldn't follow their example without displaying my holster. They kept it up, including the monkey, ignoring me completely but informing me incidentally that the squeaker was not Adrian Getz as I had first supposed, but Byram Hildebrand, Pete's coworker in the grind of drawing Dazzle Dan.

It was all very informal and homey, but I was starting to sizzle and I crossed to the far side of the room and opened a window wide. I expected an immediate reaction but got none. Disappointed at that but relieved by the rush of fresh air, I filled my chest, used my handkerchief on the brow and neck, and, turning, saw that we had company. Coming through the archway was a pink-cheeked creature in a mink coat with a dark green slab of cork or something perched on her brown hair at a cocky slant. With no one bothering to glance at her except me, she moved across toward the fireplace, slid the coat off onto a couch, displaying a tricky plaid suit with an assortment of restrained colors, and said in a. throaty voice that carried without being raised, "Rookaloo will be dead in an hour."

They were all shocked into silence except the monkey. Mrs. Koven looked at her, looked around, saw the open window, and demanded, "Who did that?"

"I did," I said manfully.

Byram Hildebrand strode to the window like a general in front of troops and pulled it shut. The monkey stopped talking and started to cough.

"Listen to him," Pete Jordan said. His baritone mellowed when he was pleased. "Pneumonia already! That's an idea! That's what I'll do when I work up to making Getz sore."

Three of them went to the cage to take a look at Rookaloo, not bothering to greet or thank her who had come just in time to save the monkey's life. She stepped to me, asking cordially, "You're Archie Goodwin? I'm Pat Lowell." She put out a hand, and I took it. She had talent as a handclasper and backed it up with a good straight look out of clear brown eyes. "I was going to phone you this morning to warn you that Mr. Koven is never ready on time for an appointment, but he arranged this himself so I didn't."

"Never again," I told her, "pass up an excuse for phoning me."

"I won't." She took her hand back and glanced at her wrist. "You're early anyway. He told us the conference would be at twelve-thirty."

"I was to come at twelve."

"Oh." She was taking me in—nothing offensive, but she sure was rating me. "To talk with him first?"

I shrugged. "I guess so."

She nodded, frowning a little. "This is a new one on me. I've been his agent and manager for three years now, handling all his business, everything from endorsements of cough drops to putting Dazzle Dan on scooters, and this is the first time a thing like this has happened, him getting someone in for a conference without consulting me —and Nero Wolfe, no less! I understand it's about a tie-up of Nero Wolfe and Dazzle Dan, having Dan start a detective agency?"

I put that question mark there, though her inflection left it to me whether to call it a question or merely a statement. I was caught off guard, so it probably showed on my face—my glee at the prospect of telling Wolfe about a tie-up between him and Dazzle Dan, with full details. I tried to erase it.

"We'd better wait," I said discreetly, "and let Mr. Koven tell it. As I understand it, I'm only here as a technical adviser, representing Mr. Wolfe because he never goes out on business. Of course you would handle the business end, and if that means you and I will have to have a lot of talks—"

I stopped because I had lost her. Her eyes were aimed past my left shoulder toward the archway, and their expression had suddenly and completely changed. They weren't exactly more alive or alert, but more concentrated. I turned, and there was Harry Koven crossing to us. His mop of black hair hadn't been combed, and he hadn't shaved. His big frame was enclosed in a red silk robe embroidered with yellow Dazzle Dans. A little guy in a dark blue suit was with him, at his elbow.

"Good morning, my little dazzlers!" Koven boomed.

"It seems cool in here," the little guy said in a gentle worried voice.

In some mysterious way the gentle little voice seemed to make more noise than the big boom. Certainly it was the gentle little voice that chopped off the return greetings from the dazzlers, but it could have been the combination of the two, the big man and the small one, that had so abruptly changed the atmosphere of the room. Before they had all been screwy perhaps, but all free and easy; now they were all tightened up. They even seemed to be tongue-tied, so I spoke.

"I opened a window," I said.

"Good heavens," the little guy mildly reproached me and trotted over to the monkey's cage. Mrs. Koven and Pete Jordan were in his path, and they hastily moved out of it, as if afraid of getting trampled, though he didn't look up to trampling anything bigger than a cricket. Not only was he too little and too old, but also he was vaguely deformed and trotted with a jerk.

Koven boomed at me, "So you got here! Don't mind the Squirt and his damn monkey. He loves that damn monkey. I call this the steam room." He let out a laugh. "How is it, Squirt, okay?"

"I think so, Harry. I hope so." The low gentle voice filled the room again.

"I hope so too, or God help Goodwin." Koven turned on Byram Hildebrand. "Has seven-twenty-eight come, By?"

"No," Hildebrand squeaked. "I phoned Furnari, and he said it would be right over."

"Late again. We may have to change. When it comes, do a revise on the third frame. Where Dan says, 'Not to-night, my dear,' make it, 'Not today, my dear.' Got it?"

"But we discussed that—"

"I know, but change it. We'll change seven-twenty-nine to fit. Have you finished seven-thirty-three?"

"No. It's only—"

"Then what are you doing up here?"

"Why, Goodwin came, and you said you wanted us at twelve-thirty—"

"I'll let you know when we're ready—sometime after lunch. Show me the revise on seven-twenty-eight." Koven glanced around masterfully. "How is everybody? Blooming? See you all later. Come along, Goodwin, sorry you had to wait. Come with me."

He headed for the archway, and I followed, across the hall and up the next flight of stairs. There the arrangement was different; instead of a big square hall there was a narrow corridor with four doors, all closed. He turned left, to the door at that end, opened it, held it for me to pass through, and shut it again. This room was an improvement in several ways: it was ten degrees cooler, it had no monkey, and the furniture left more room to move around. The most prominent item was a big old scarred desk over by a window. After inviting me to sit, Koven went and sat at the desk and removed covers from dishes that were there on a tray.

"Breakfast," he said. "You had yours."

It wasn't a question, but I said yes to be sociable. He needed all the sociability he could get, from the looks of the tray. There was one dejected poached egg, one wavy thin piece of toast, three undersized prunes with about a teaspoonful of juice, a split of tonic water, and a glass. It was an awful sight. He waded into the prunes. When they were gone he poured the tonic water into the glass, took a sip, and demanded, "Did you bring it?"

"The gun? Sure."

"Let me see it."

"It's the one we showed you at the office." I moved to another chair, closer to him. "I'm supposed to check with you before we proceed. Is that the desk you kept your gun in?"

He nodded and swallowed a nibble of toast. "Here in this left-hand drawer, in the back."

"Loaded."

"Yes. I told you so."

"So you did. You also told us that you bought it two years ago in Montana, when you were there at a dude

ranch, and brought it home with you and never bothered
to get a license for it, and it's been there in the drawer
right along. You saw it there a week or ten days ago, and
last Friday you saw it was gone. You didn't want to call
the cops for two reasons, because you have no license for
it, and because you think it was taken by one of the five
people whose names you gave—"

"I think it may have been."

"You didn't put it like that. However, skip it. You gave
us the five names. By the way, was that Adrian Getz, the
one you called Squirt?"

"Yes."

"Then they're all five here, and we can go ahead and
get it over with. As I understand it, I am to put my gun
there in the drawer where yours was, and you get them
up here for a conference, with me present. You were to
cook up something to account for me. Have you done
that?"

He swallowed another nibble of toast and egg. Wolfe
would have had that meal down in five seconds flat—or
rather, he would have had it out the window. "I thought
this might do," Koven said. "I can say that I'm considering a new stunt for Dan, have him start a detective agency,
and I've called Nero Wolfe in for consultation, and he
sent you up for a conference. We can discuss it a little,
and I ask you to show us how a detective searches a room
to give us an idea of the picture potential. You shouldn't
start with the desk; start maybe with the shelves back
of me. When you come to do the desk I'll push my chair
back to be out of your way, and I'll have them right in
front of me. When you open the drawer and take the gun
out and they see it—"

"I thought you were going to do that."

"I know, that's what I said, but this is better because
this way they'll be looking at the gun and you, and I'll be
watching their faces. I'll have my eye right on them, and
the one that took my gun, if one of them did it—when he
or she suddenly sees you pull a gun out of the drawer
that's exactly like it, it's going to show on his face, and I'm
going to see it. We'll do it that way."

I admit it sounded better there on the spot than it had in Wolfe's office—and besides, he had revised it. This way he might really get what he wanted. I considered it, watching him finish the tonic water. The toast and egg were gone.

"It sounds all right," I conceded, "except for one thing. You'll be expecting a look of surprise, but what if there are five looks of surprise? At seeing me take a gun out of your desk—those who don't know you had a gun there."

"But they do know."

"All of them?"

"Certainly. I thought I told you that. Anyhow, they all know. Everybody knows everything around this place. They thought I ought to get rid of it, and now I wish I had. You understand, Goodwin, all there is to this—I just want to know where the damn thing is, I want to know who took it, and I'll handle it myself from there. I told Wolfe that."

"I know you did." I got up and went to his side of the desk, at his left, and pulled a drawer open. "In here?"

"Yes."

"The rear compartment?"

"Yes."

I reached to my holster for the Marley, broke it, removed the cartridges and dropped them into my vest pocket, put the gun in the drawer, shut the drawer, and returned to my chair.

"Okay," I said, "get them up here. We can ad lib it all right without any rehearsing."

He looked at me. He opened the drawer for a peek at the gun, not touching it, and pushed the drawer to. He shoved the tray away, leaned back, and began working on his upper lip with the jagged yellow teeth.

"I'm going to have to get my nerve up," he said, as if appealing to me. "I'm never much good until late afternoon."

I grunted. "What the hell. You told me to be here at noon and called the conference for twelve-thirty."

"I know I did. I do things like that." He chewed the lip some more. "And I've got to dress." Suddenly his voice went high in protest. "Don't try to rush me, understand?"

I was fed up, but had already invested a lot of time and a dollar for a taxi on the case, so kept calm. "I know," I told him, "artists are temperamental. But I'll explain how Mr. Wolfe charges. He sets a fee, depending on the job, and if it takes more of my time than he thinks reason- able he adds an extra hundred dollars an hour. Keeping me here until late afternoon would be expensive. I could go and come back."

He didn't like that and said so, explaining why, the idea being that with me there in the house it would be easier for him to get his nerve up and it might only take an hour or so. He got up and walked to the door and opened it, then turned and demanded, "Do you know how much I make an hour? The time I spend on my work? Over a thousand dollars. More than a thousand an hour! I'll go get some clothes on."

He went, shutting the door.

My wristwatch said 1:17. My stomach agreed. I sat maybe ten minutes, then went to the phone on the desk, dialed, got Wolfe, and told him how it was. He told me to go out and get some lunch, naturally, and I said I would, but after hanging up I went back to my chair. If I went out, sure as hell Koven would get his nerve up in my absence, and by the time I got back he would have lost it again and have to start over. I explained the situation to my stomach, and it made a polite sound of protest, but I was the boss. I was glancing at my watch again and seeing 1:42 when the door opened and Mrs. Koven was with me.

When I stood, her serious gray eyes beneath the wide smooth brow were level with the knot in my four-in-hand. She said her husband had told her that I was staying for a conference at a later hour. I confirmed it. She said I ought to have something to eat. I agreed that it was not a bad notion.

"Won't you," she invited, "come down and have a sand- wich with us? We don't do any cooking, we even have our breakfast sent in, but there are some sandwiches."

"I don't want to be rude," I told her, "but are they in the room with the monkey?"

"Oh, no." She stayed serious. "Wouldn't that be awful? Downstairs in the workroom." She touched my arm. "Come on, do."

I went downstairs with her.

II

IN A large room at the rear on the ground floor the other four suspects were seated around a plain wooden table, dealing with the sandwiches. The room was a mess—drawing tables under fluorescent lights, open shelves crammed with papers, cans of all sizes, and miscellaneous objects, chairs scattered around, other shelves with books and portfolios, and tables with more stacks of papers. Messy as it was to the eye, it was even messier to the ear, for two radios were going full blast.

Marcelle Koven and I joined them at the lunch table, and I perked up at once. There was a basket of French bread and pumpernickel, paper platters piled with slices of ham, smoked turkey, sturgeon, and hot corned beef, a big slab of butter, mustard and other accessories, bottles of milk, a pot of steaming coffee, and a one-pound jar of fresh caviar. Seeing Pete Jordan spooning caviar onto a piece of bread crust, I got what he meant about liking to eat.

"Help yourself!" Pat Lowell yelled into my ear.

I reached for the bread with one hand and the corned beef with the other and yelled back, "Why doesn't someone turn them down or even off?"

She took a sip of coffee from a paper cup and shook her head. "One's By Hildebrand's and one's Pete Jordan's! They like different programs when they're working! They have to go for volume!"

It was a hell of a din, but the corned beef was wonderful and the bread must have been from Rusterman's, nor was there anything wrong with the turkey and sturgeon. Since the radio duel precluded table talk, I used my eyes for diversion and was impressed by Adrian Getz, whom Koven called the Squirt. He would break off a rectangle of bread crust, place a rectangle of sturgeon on it, arrange a mound of caviar on top, and pop it in. When it was down he would take three sips of coffee and then start over. He was doing that when Mrs. Koven and I arrived and he was still doing it when I was full and reaching for another paper napkin.

Eventually, though, he stopped. He pushed back his chair, left it, went over to a sink at the wall, held his fingers under the faucet, and dried them with his handkerchief. Then he trotted over to a radio and turned it off, and to the other one and turned that off. Then he trotted back to us and spoke apologetically.

"That was uncivil, I know."

No one contradicted him.

"It was only," he went on, "that I wanted to ask Mr. Goodwin something before going up for my nap." His eyes settled on me. "Did you know when you opened that window that sudden cold drafts are dangerous for tropical monkeys?"

His tone was more than mild, it was wistful. But something about him—I didn't know what and didn't ask for time out to go into it—got my goat.

"Sure," I said cheerfully. "I was trying it out."

"That was thoughtless," he said, not complaining, just giving his modest opinion, and turned and trotted out of the room.

There was a strained silence. Pat Lowell reached for the pot to pour some coffee.

"Goodwin, God help you," Pete Jordan muttered.

"Why? Does he sting?"

"Don't ask me why, but watch your step. I think he's a kobold." He tossed his paper napkin onto the table. "Want to see an artist create? Come and look." He marched to one of the radios and turned it on, then to a drawing table and sat.

"I'll clean up," Pat Lowell offered.

Byram Hildebrand, who had not squeaked once that I heard, went and turned on the other radio before he took his place at another drawing table.

Mrs. Koven left us. I helped Pat Lowell clear up the

lunch table, but all that did was pass time, since both
radios were going and I rely mostly on talk to develop an
acquaintance in the early stages. Then she left, and I
strolled over to watch the artists. So far nothing had oc-
cured to change my opinion of Dazzle Dan, but I had
to admire the way they did him. Working from rough
sketches which all looked alike to me, they turned out
the finished product in three colors so fast I could barely
keep up, walking back and forth. The only interruptions
for a long stretch were when Hildebrand jumped up to
go and turn his radio louder, and a minute later Pete
Jordan did likewise. I sat down and concentrated on the
experiment of listening to two stations at once, but after
a while my brain started to curdle and I got out of there.

A door toward the front of the lower hall was standing
open, and I looked in and stepped inside when I saw Pat
Lowell at a desk, working with papers. She looked up to
nod and went on working.

"Listen a minute," I said. "We're here on a desert
island, and for months you have been holding me at arm's
length, and I'm desperate. It is not mere propinquity. In
rags and tatters as you are, without make-up, I have come
to look upon you—"

"I'm busy," she said emphatically. "Go play with a
coconut."

"You'll regret this," I said savagely and went to the hall
and looked through the glass of the front door at the outside world. The view was nothing to brag about, and the
radios were still at my eardrums, so I went upstairs. Looking through the archway into the room at the left, and
seeing no one but the monkey in its cage, I crossed to the
other room and entered. It was full of furniture, but there
was no sign of life. As I went up the second flight of stairs
it seemed that the sound of the radios was getting louder
instead of softer, and at the top I knew why. A radio was
going the other side of one of the closed doors. I went
and opened the door to the room where I had talked with
Koven; not there. I tried another door and was faced by
shelves stacked with linen. I knocked on another, got no
response, opened it, and stepped in. It was a large bed-

room, very fancy, with an oversized bed. The furniture and fiittings showed that it was co-ed. A radio on a stand was giving with a soap opera, and stretched out on a couch was Mrs. Koven, sound asleep. She looked softer and not so serious, with her lips parted a little and relaxed fingers curled on the cushion, in spite of the yapping radio on the bedside table. I damn well intended to find Koven, and took a couple of steps with a vague notion of looking under the bed for him, when a glance through an open door at the right into the next room discovered him. He was standing at a window with his back to me. Thinking it might seem a little familiar on short acquaintance for me to enter from the bedroom where his wife was snoozing, I backed out to the hall, pulling the door to, moved to the next door, and knocked. Getting no reaction, I turned the knob and entered.

The radio had drowned out my noise. He remained at the window. I banged the door shut. He jerked around. He said something, but I didn't get it on account of the radio. I went and closed the door to the bedroom, and that helped some.

"Well?" he demanded, as if he couldn't imagine who I was or what I wanted.

He had shaved and combed and had on a well-made brown homespun suit, with a tan shirt and red tie.

"It's going on four o'clock," I said, "and I'll be going soon and taking my gun with me."

He took his hands from his pockets and dropped into a chair. Evidently this was the Koven personal living room, from the way it was furnished, and it looked fairly livable.

He spoke. "I was standing at the window thinking."

"Yeah. Any luck?"

He sighed and stretched his legs out. "Fame and fortune," he said, "are not all a man needs for happiness."

I sat down. Obviously the only alternatives were to wrangle him into it or call it off.

"What else would you suggest?" I asked brightly.

He undertook to tell me. He went on and on, but I won't report it verbatim because I doubt if it contained any helpful hints for you—I know it didn't for me.

I grunted from time to time to be polite. I listened to him for a while and then got a little relief by listening to the soap opera on the radio, which was muffled some by the closed door but by no means inaudible. Eventually, of course, he got around to his wife, first briefing me by explaining that she was his third and they had been married only two years. To my surprise he didn't tear her apart. He said she was wonderful. His point was that even when you added to fame and fortune the companionship of a beloved and loving wife who was fourteen years younger than you, that still wasn't all you needed for happiness.

There was one interruption—a knock on the door and the appearance of Byram Hildebrand. He had come to show the revise on the third frame of Number 728. They discussed art some, and Koven okayed the revise, and Hildebrand departed. I hoped that the intermission had sidetracked Koven, but no; he took up again where he had left off.

I can take a lot when I'm working on a case, even a kindergarten problem like that one, but finally, after the twentieth sidewise glance at my wrist, I called a halt.

"Look," I said, "this has given me a new slant on life entirely, and don't think I don't appreciate it, but it's a quarter past four and it's getting dark. I would call it late afternoon. What do you say we go ahead with our act?"

He closed his trap and frowned at me. He started chewing his lip. After some of that he suddenly arose, went to a cabinet, and got out a bottle.

"Will you join me?" He produced two glasses. "I'm not supposed to drink until five o'clock, but I'll make this an exception." He came to me. "Bourbon all right? Say when."

I would have liked to plug him. He had known from the beginning that he would have to drink himself up to it but had sucked me in with a noon appointment. Anything I felt like saying would have been justified, but I held in. I accepted mine and raised it with him, to encourage him, and took a swallow. He took a dainty sip, raised his eyes to the ceiling, and then emptied the glass at a gulp. He picked up the bottle and poured a refill.

"Why don't we go in there with the refreshment," I sugested, "and go over it a little?"

"Don't rush me," he said gloomily. He took a deep breath, swelling his chest, and suddenly grinned at me, showing the teeth. He lifted the glass and drained it, reached for the bottle and tilted it to pour, and changed his mind.

"Come on," he said, heading for the door. I stepped around him to open the door, since both his hands were occupied, closed it behind us, and followed him down the hall. At the farther end we entered the room where we were to stage it. He went to the desk and sat, poured himself a drink, and put the bottle down. I went to the desk too, but not to sit. I had taken the precaution of removing the cartridges from my gun, but even so a glance at it wouldn't hurt any. I pulled the drawer open and was relieved to see that it was still there. I shut the drawer.

"I'll go get them," I offered.

"I said don't rush me," Koven protested, but no longer gloomy.

Thinking that two more drinks would surely do it, I moved to a chair. But I didn't sit. Something wasn't right, and it came to me what it was: I had placed the gun with the muzzle pointing to the right, and it wasn't that way now. I returned to the desk, took the gun out, and gave it a look.

It was a Marley .32 all right, but not mine.

III

I PUT my eye on Koven. The gun was in my left hand, and my right hand was a fist. If I had hit him that first second, which I nearly did, mad as I was, I would have cracked some knuckles.

"What's the matter?" he demanded.

My eyes were on him and through him. I kept them there for five pulse beats. It wasn't possible, I decided, that he was that good. Nobody could be.

I backed up a pace. "We've found your gun."

He gawked at me. "What?"

I broke it, saw that the cylinder was empty, and held it out. "Take a look."

He took it. "It looks the same—no, it doesn't."

"Certainly it doesn't. Mine was clean and bright. Is it yours?"

"I don't know. It looks like it. But how in the name of God—"

I reached and took it from him. "How do you think?" I was so damn mad I nearly stuttered. "Someone with hands took mine out and put yours in. It could have been you. Was it?"

"No. Me?" Suddenly he got indignant. "How the hell could it have been me when I didn't know where mine was?"

"You said you didn't. I ought to stretch you out and tamp you down. Keeping me here the whole goddam day, and now this! If you ever talk straight and to the point, now is the time. Did you touch my gun?"

"No. But you're—"

"Do you know who did?"

"No. But you're—"

"Shut up!" I went around the desk to the phone, lifted it, and dialed. At that hour Wolfe would be up in the plant rooms for his afternoon shift with the orchids, where he was not to be disturbed except in emergency, but this was one. When Fritz answered I asked him to buzz the extension, and in a moment I had Wolfe.

"Yes, Archie?" Naturally he was peevish.

"Sorry to bother you, but I'm at Koven's. I put my gun in his desk, and we were all set for his stunt, but he kept putting it off until now. His will power sticks and has to be primed with alcohol. I roamed around. We just came in here where his desk is, and I opened the drawer for a look. Someone has taken my gun and substituted his— his that was stolen, you know? It's back where it belongs, but mine is gone."

"You shouldn't have left it there."

"Okay, you can have that, and you sure will, but I need

instructions for now. Three choices: I can call a cop, or I can bring the whole bunch down there to you, don't think I can't the way I feel, or I can handle it myself. Which?"

"Confound it, not the police. They would enjoy it too much. And why bring them here? The gun's there, not here."

"Then that leaves me. I go ahead?"

"Certainly—with due discretion. It's a prank." He chuckled. "I would like to see your face. Try to get home for dinner." He hung up.

"My God, don't call a cop!" Koven protested.

"I don't intend to," I said grimly. I slipped his gun into my armpit holster. "Not if I can help it. It depends partly on you. You stay put, right here. I'm going down and get them. Your wife's asleep in the bedroom. If I find when I get back that you've gone and started chatting with her I'll either slap you down with your own gun or phone the police, I don't know which, maybe both. Stay put."

"This is my house, Goodwin, and—"

"Goddam it, don't you know a raving maniac when you see one?" I tapped my chest with a forefinger. "Me. When I'm as sore as I am now the safest thing would be for you to call a cop. I want my gun."

As I made for the door he was reaching for the bottle. By the time I got down to the ground floor I had myself well enough in hand to speak to them without betraying any special urgency, telling them that Koven was ready for them upstairs, for the conference. I found Pat Lowell still at the desk in the room in front and Hildebrand and Jordan still at their drawing tables in the workroom. I even replied appropriately when Pat Lowell asked how I had made out with the coconut. As Hildebrand and Jordan left their tables and turned off their radios I had a keener eye on them than before; someone here had swiped my gun. As we ascended the first flight of stairs, with me in the rear, I asked their backs where I would find Adrian Getz.

Pat Lowell answered. "He may be in his room on the top floor." They halted at the landing, the edge of the big square hall, and I joined them. We could hear the radio going upstairs. She indicated the room to the left. "He takes his afternoon nap in there with Rookaloo, but not this late usually."

I thought I might as well glance in, and moved to the archway. A draft of cold air hit me, and I went on in. A window was wide open! I marched over and closed it, then went to take a look at the monkey. It was huddled on the floor in a corner of the cage, making angry little noises, with something clutched in its fingers against its chest. The light was dim, but I have good eyes, and not only was the something unmistakably a gun, but it was my Marley on a bet. Needing light, and looking for a wall switch, I was passing the large couch which faced the fireplace when suddenly I stopped and froze. Adrian Getz, the Squirt, was lying on the couch but he wasn't taking a nap.

I bent over him for a close-up and saw a hole in his skull northeast of his right ear, and some red juice. I stuck a hand inside the V of his vest and flattened it against him and held my breath for eight seconds. He was through taking naps.

I straightened up and called, "Come in here, all three of you, and switch on a light as you come!"

They appeared through the archway, and one of them put a hand to the wall. Lights shone. The back of the couch hid Getz from their view as they approached.

"It's cold in here," Pat Lowell was saying. "Did you open another—"

Seeing Getz stopped her, and the others too. They goggled.

"Don't touch him," I warned them. "He's dead, so you can't help him any. Don't touch anything. You three stay here together, right here in this room, while I—"

"Christ Almighty," Pete Jordan blurted. Hildebrand squeaked something. Pat Lowell put out a hand, found the couch back, and gripped it. She asked something, but I wasn't listening. I was at the cage, with my back to them, peering at the monkey. It was my Marley the monkey was clutching. I had to curl my fingers until the nails sank in to keep from opening the cage door and grabbing that gun.

I whirled. "Stick here together. Understand?" I was on my way. "I'm going up and phone."

Ignoring their noises, I left them. I mounted the stairs in no hurry, because if I had been a raving maniac before, I was now stiff with fury and I needed a few seconds to get under control. In the room upstairs Harry Koven was still seated at the desk, staring at the open drawer. He looked up and fired a question at me but got no answer. I went to the phone, lifted it, and dialed a number. When I got Wolfe he started to sputter at being disturbed again.

"I'm sorry," I told him, "but I wish to report that I have found my gun. It's in the cage with the monkey, who is—"

"What monkey?"

"Its name is Rookaloo, but please don't interrupt. It is holding my gun to its breast, I suspect because it is cold and the gun is warm, having recently been fired. Lying there on a couch is the body of a man, Adrian Getz, with a bullet hole in the head. It is no longer a question whether I call a cop, I merely wanted to report the situation to you before I do so. A thousand to one Getz was shot and killed with my gun. I will not be—hold it—"

I dropped the phone and jumped. Koven had made a dive for the door. I caught him before he reached it, got an arm and his chin, and heaved. There was a lot of feeling in it, and big as he was he sailed to a wall, bounced off, and went to the floor.

"I would love to do it again," I said, meaning it, and returned to the phone and told Wolfe, "Excuse me, Koven tried to interrupt. I was only going to say I will not be home to dinner."

"The man is dead."

"Yes, sir."

"Have you anything satisfactory for the police?"

"Sure. My apologies for bringing my gun here to oblige a murderer. That's all."

"We haven't answered today's mail."

"I know. It's a damn shame. I'll get away as soon as I can."

"Very well."

The connection went. I held the button down a moment, with an eye on Koven, who was upright again but not asking for an encore, then released it and dialed RE 7-5260.

IV

I HAVEN'T kept anything like an accurate score, but I would say that over the years I haven't told the cops more than a couple of dozen barefaced lies, maybe not that many. They are seldom practical. On the other hand, I can't recall any murder case Wolfe and I were in on and I've had my story gone into at length where I have simply opened the bag and given them all I had, with no dodging and no withholding, except one, and this is it. On the murder of Adrian Getz I didn't have a single thing on my mind that I wasn't willing and eager to shovel out, so I let them have it.

It worked fine. They called me a liar.

Not right away, of course. At first even Inspector Cramer appreciated my cooperation, knowing as he did that there wasn't a man in his army who could shade me at seeing and hearing, remembering, and reporting. It was generously conceded that upon finding the body I had performed properly and promptly, herding the trio into the room and keeping the Kovens from holding a family council until the law arrived. From there on, of course, everyone had been under surveillance, including me.

At six-thirty, when the scientists were still monopolizing the room where Getz had got it, and city employees were wandering all over the place, and the various inmates were still in various rooms conversing privately with Homicide men, and I had typed and signed my own frank and full statement, I was confidently expecting that I would soon be out on the sidewalk unattended, flagging a taxi. I was in the front room on the ground floor, seated at Pat Lowell's desk, having used her typewriter, and Sergeant Purley Stebbins was sitting across from me, looking over my statement.

He lifted his head and regarded me, perfectly friendly. A perfectly friendly look from Stebbins would, from almost anyone else, cause you to get your guard up and be ready to either duck or counter, but Purley wasn't responsible for the design of his big bony face and his pig-bristle eyebrows.

"I guess you got it all in," he admitted. "As you told it."

"I suggest," I said modestly, "that when this case is put away you send that to the school to be used as a model report."

"Yeah." He stood up. "You're a good typist." He turned to go.

I arose too, saying casually, "I can run along now?"

The door opened, and Inspector Cramer entered. I didn't like his expression as he darted a glance at me. Knowing him well in all his moods, I didn't like the way his broad shoulders were hunched, or his clamped jaw, or the glint in his eye.

"Here's Goodwin's statement," Purley said. "Okay."

"As he told it?"

"Yes."

"Send him downtown and hold him."

It caught me completely off balance. "Hold *me?*" I demanded, squeaking almost like Hildebrand.

"Yes, sir." Nothing could catch Purley off balance. "On your order?"

"No, charge him. Sullivan Act. He has no license for the gun we found on him."

"Ha, ha," I said. "Ha, ha, and ha, ha. There, you got your laugh. A very fine gag. Ha."

"You're going down, Goodwin. I'll be down to see you later."

As I said, I knew him well. He meant it. I had his eyes. "This," I said, "is way out of my reach. I've told you where and how and why I got that gun." I pointed to the paper in Purley's hand. "Read it. It's all down, punctuated."

"You had the gun in your holster and you have no license for it."

"Nuts. But I get it. You've been hoping for years to hang something on Nero Wolfe, and to you I'm just a part of him, and you think here's your chance. Of course it won't stick. Wouldn't you rather have something that will? Like resisting arrest and assaulting an officer? Glad to oblige. Watch it—"

Tipping forward, I started a left hook for his jaw, fast and vicious, then jerked it down and went back on my heels. It didn't create a panic, but I had the satisfaction of seeing Cramer take a quick step back and Stebbins one forward. They bumped.

"There," I said. "With both of you to swear to it, that ought to be good for at least two years. I'll throw the typewriter at you if you'll promise to catch it."

"Cut the clowning," Purley growled.

"You lied about that gun," Cramer snapped. "If you don't want to get taken down to think it over, think now. Tell me what you came here for and what happened."

"I've told you."

"A string of lies."

"No, sir."

"You can have 'em back. I'm not trying to hang something on Wolfe, or you either. I want to know why you came here and what happened."

"Oh, for God's sake." I moved my eyes. "Okay, Purley, where's my escort?"

Cramer strode four paces to the door, opened it, and called, "Bring Mr. Koven in here!"

Harry Koven entered with a dick at his elbow. He looked as if he was even farther away from happiness than before.

"We'll sit down," Cramer said.

He left me behind the desk. Purley and the dick took chairs in the background. Cramer stationed himself across the desk from me, where Purley had been, with Koven on a chair at his left. He opened up.

"I told you, Mr. Koven, that I would ask you to repeat your story in Goodwin's presence, and you said you would."

Koven nodded. "That's right." He was hoarse.

"We won't need all the details. Just answer me briefly. When you called on Nero Wolfe last Saturday evening, what did you ask him to do?"

"I told him I was going to have Dazzle Dan start a detective agency in a new series." The hoarseness bothered Koven, and he cleared his throat explosively. "I told him I needed technical assistance, and possibly a tie-up, if we could arrange—"

There was a pad of ruled paper on the desk. I reached for it, and a pencil, and started doing shorthand. Cramer leaned over, stretched an arm, grabbed a corner of the pad, and jerked it away. I could feel the blood coming to my head, which was silly of it with an inspector, a sergeant, and a private all in the room.

"We need your full attention," Cramer growled. He went to Koven. "Did you say anything to Wolfe about your gun being taken from your desk?"

"Certainly not. It hadn't been taken. I did mention that I had a gun in my desk for which I had no license, but that I never carried it, and I asked if that was risky. I told them what make it was, a Marley thirty-two. I asked how much trouble it would be to get a license, and if—"

"We'll keep it brief. Just cover the points. What arrangement did you make with Wolfe?"

"He agreed to send Goodwin to my place on Monday for a conference with my staff and me."

"About what?"

"About the technical problems of having Dazzle Dan do detective work, and possibly a tie-up."

"And Goodwin came?"

"Yes, today around noon." Koven's hoarseness kept interfering with him, and he kept clearing his throat. My eyes were at his face, but he hadn't met them. Of course he was talking to Cramer and had to be polite. He went on, "The conference was for twelve-thirty, but I had a little talk with Goodwin and asked him to wait. I have to be careful what I do with Dan and I wanted to think it over some more. Anyway I'm like that, I put things off. It was after four o'clock when he—"

"Was your talk with Goodwin about your gun being gone?"

"Certainly not. We might have mentioned the gun, about my not having a license for it, I don't remember—

no, wait a minute, we must have, because I pulled the drawer open and we glanced in at it. Except for that, we only talked—"

"Did you or Goodwin take your gun out of the drawer?"

"No. Absolutely not."

"Did he put his gun in the drawer?"

"Absolutely not."

I slid in, "When I took my gun from my holster to show it to you, did you—"

"Nothing doing," Cramer snapped at me. "You're listening. Just the high spots for now." He returned to Koven. "Did you have another talk with Goodwin later?"

Koven nodded. "Yes, around half-past three he came up to my room—the living room. We talked until after four, there and in my office, and then—"

"In your office did Goodwin open the drawer of the desk and take the gun out and say it had been changed?"

"Certainly not!"

"What did he do?"

"Nothing, only we talked, and then he left to go down and get the others to come up for the conference. After a while he came back alone, and without saying anything he came to the desk and took my gun from the drawer and put it under his coat. Then he went to the phone and called Nero Wolfe. When I heard him tell Wolfe that Adrian Getz had been shot, that he was on a couch downstairs dead, I got up to go down there, and Goodwin jumped me from behind and knocked me out. When I came to he was still talking to Wolfe, I don't know what he was telling him, and then he called the police. He wouldn't let me—"

"Hold it," Cramer said curtly. "That covers that. One more point. Do you know of any motive for Goodwin's wanting to murder Adrian Getz?"

"No, I don't. I told—"

"Then if Getz was shot with Goodwin's gun how would you account for it? You're not obliged to account for it, but if you don't mind just repeat what you told me."

"Well—" Koven hesitated. He cleared his throat for the twentieth time. "I told you about the monkey. Goodwin opened a window, and that's enough to kill that kind of a monkey, and Getz was very fond of it. He didn't show how upset he was but Getz was very quiet and didn't show things much. I understand Goodwin likes to kid people. Of course I don't know what happened, but if Goodwin went in there later when Getz was there, and started to open a window, you can't tell. When Getz once got aroused he was apt to do anything. He couldn't have hurt Goodwin any, but Goodwin might have got out his gun just for a gag, and Getz tried to take it away, and it went off accidentally. That wouldn't be murder, would it?"

"No," Cramer said, "that would only be a regrettable accident. That's all for now, Mr. Koven. Take him out, Sol, and bring Hildebrand."

As Koven arose and the dick came forward I reached for the phone on Pat Lowell's desk. My hand got there, but so did Cramer's, hard on top of mine.

"The lines here are busy," he stated. "There'll be a phone you can use downtown. Do you want to hear Hildebrand before you comment?"

"I'm crazy to hear Hildebrand," I assured him. "No doubt he'll explain that I tossed the gun in the monkey's cage to frame the monkey. Let's just wait for Hildebrand."

It wasn't much of a wait; the Homicide boys are snappy. Byram Hildebrand, ushered in by Sol, stood and gave me a long straight look before he took the chair Koven had vacated. He still had good presence, with his fine mat of nearly white hair, but his extremities were nervous. When he sat he couldn't find comfortable spots for either his hands or his feet.

"This will only take a minute," Cramer told him. "I just want to check on Sunday morning. Yesterday. You were here working?"

Hildebrand nodded, and the squeak came. "I was putting on some touches. I often work Sundays."

"You were in there in the workroom?"

"Yes. Mr. Getz was there, making some suggestions. I was doubtful about one of his suggestions and went upstairs to consult Mr. Koven, but Mrs. Koven was there in the hall and—"

"You mean the big hall one flight up?"

"Yes. She said Mr. Koven wasn't up yet and Miss Lowell was in his office waiting to see him. Miss Lowell has extremely good judgment, and I went up to consult her. She disapproved of Mr. Getz's suggestion, and we discussed various matters, and mention was made of the gun Mr. Koven kept in his desk drawer. I pulled the drawer open just to look at it, with no special purpose, merely to look at it, and closed the drawer again. Shortly afterward I returned downstairs."

"Was the gun there in the drawer?"

"Yes."

"Did you take it out?"

"No. Neither did Miss Lowell. We didn't touch it."

"But you recognized it as the same gun?"

"I can't say that I did, no. I had never examined the gun, never had it in my hand. I can only say that it looked the same as before. It was my opinion that our concern about the gun being kept there was quite childish, but I see now that I was wrong. After what happened today—"

"Yeah." Cramer cut him off. "Concern about a loaded gun is never childish. That's all I'm after now. Sunday morning, in Miss Lowell's presence, you opened the drawer of Koven's desk and saw the gun which you took to be the gun you had seen there before. Is that correct?"

"That's correct," Hildebrand squeaked.

"Okay, that's all." Cramer nodded at Sol. "Take him back to Rowcliff."

I treated myself to a good deep breath. Purley was squinting at me, not gloating, just concentrating. Cramer turned his head to see that the door was closed after the dick and the artist and then turned back to me.

"Your turn," he growled.

I shook my head. "Lost my voice," I whispered, hissing.

"You're not funny, Goodwin. You're never as funny as you think you are. This time you're not funny at all. You can have five minutes to go over it and realize how complicated it is. When you phoned Wolfe before you phoned us, you couldn't possibly have arranged all the details. I've got you. I'll be leaving here before long to join you downtown, and on my way I'll stop in at Wolfe's place for a talk. He won't clam up on this one. At the very least I've got you good on the Sullivan Act. Want five minutes?"

"No, sir." I was calm but emphatic. "I want five days and I would advise you to take a full week. Complicated doesn't begin to describe it. Before I leave for downtown, if you're actually going to crawl out on that one, I wish to remind you of something, and don't forget it. When I voluntarily took Koven's gun from my holster and turned it over—it wasn't 'found on me,' as you put it—I also turned over six nice clean cartridges which I had in my vest pocket, having previously removed them from my gun. I hope none of your heroes gets careless and mixes them up with the cartridges found in my gun, if any, when you retrieved it from the monkey. That would be a mistake. The point is, if I removed the cartridges from my gun in order to insert one or more from Koven's gun, when and why did I do it? There's a day's work for you right there. And if I did do it, then Koven's friendly effort to fix me up for justifiable manslaughter is wasted, much as I appreciate it, because I must have been premeditating something, and you know what. Why fiddle around with the Sullivan Act? Make it the big one, and I can't get bail. Now I button up."

I set my jaw.

Cramer eyed me. "Even a suspended sentence," he said, "you lose your license."

I grinned at him.

"You goddam mule," Purley rumbled.

I included him in the grin.

"Send him down," Cramer rasped and got up and left.

V

EVEN when a man is caught smack in the middle of a felony, as I had been, there is a certain amount of red tape to getting him behind bars, and in my case not only red tape but also other activities postponed my attainment of privacy. First I had a long conversation with an assistant district attorney, who was the suave and subtle type and even ate sandwiches with me. When it was over, a little after nine o'clock, both of us were only slightly more confused than when we started. He left me in a room with a specimen in uniform with slick brown hair and a wart on his cheek. I told him how to get rid of the wart, recommending Doc Vollmer.

I was expecting the promised visit by Inspector Cramer any minute. Naturally I was nursing an assorted collection of resentments, but the one on top was at not being there to see and hear the talk between Cramer and Wolfe. Any chat those two had was always worth listening to, and that one must have been outstanding, with Wolfe learning not only that his client was lying five ways from Sunday, which was bad enough, but also that I had been tossed in the can and the day's mail would have to go unanswered.

When the door finally opened and a visitor entered it wasn't Inspector Cramer. It was Lieutenant Rowcliff, whose murder I will not have to premeditate when I get around to it because I have already done the premeditating. There are not many murderers so vicious and inhuman that I would enjoy seeing them caught by Rowcliff. He jerked a chair around to sit facing me and said with oily satisfaction, "At last we've got you, by God."

That set the tone of the interview.

I would enjoy recording in full that two-hour session with Rowcliff, but it would sound like bragging, and therefore I don't suppose you would enjoy it too. His biggest handicap is that when he gets irritated to a certain point he can't help stuttering, and I'm onto him enough to tell when he's just about there, and then I start stuttering before he does. Even with a close watch and careful timing it takes luck to do it right, and that evening I was lucky. He came closer than ever before to plugging me, but didn't, because he wants to be a captain so bad he can taste it and he's not absolutely sure that Wolfe hasn't got a solid in with the Commissioner or the Mayor or possibly Grover Whalen himself.

Cramer never showed up, and that added another resentment to my healthy pile. I knew he had been to see Wolfe, because when they had finally let me make my phone call, around eight o'clock, and I had got Wolfe and started to tell him about it, he had interrupted me in a voice as cold as an Eskimo's nose.

"I know where you are and how you got there. Mr. Cramer is here. I have phoned Mr. Parker, but it's too late to do anything tonight. Have you had anything to eat?"

"No, sir. I'm afraid of poison and I'm on a hunger strike."

"You should eat something. Mr. Cramer is worse than a jackass, he's demented. I intend to persuade him, if possible, of the desirability of releasing you at once."

He hung up.

When, shortly after eleven, Rowcliff called it off and I was shown to my room, there had been no sign of Cramer. The room was in no way remarkable, merely what was to be expected in a structure of that type, but it was fairly clean, strongly scented with disinfectant, and was in a favorable location since the nearest corridor light was six paces away and therefore did not glare through the bars of my door. Also it was a single, which I appreciated. Alone at last, away from telephones and other interruptions, I undressed and arranged my gray pinstripe on the chair, draped my shirt over the end of the blankets, got in, stretched, and settled down for a complete survey of the complications. But my brain and nerves had other plans, and in twenty seconds I was asleep.

In the morning there was a certain amount of activity, with the check-off and a trip to the lavatory and breakfast, but after that I had more privacy than I really cared for. My watch had slowed down. I tested the second hand by counting, with no decisive result. By noon I would almost have welcomed a visit from Rowcliff and was beginning to suspect that someone had lost a paper and there was no record of me anywhere and everyone was too busy to stop and think. Lunch, which I will not describe, broke the monotony some, but then, back in my room, I was alone with my wristwatch. For the tenth time I decided to spread all the pieces out, sort them, and have a look at the picture as it had been drawn to date, and for the tenth time it got so damn jumbled that I couldn't make first base, let alone on around.

At 1:09 my door swung open and the floorwalker, a chunky short guy with only half an ear on the right side, told me to come along. I went willingly, on out of the block to an elevator, and along a ground-floor corridor to an office. There I was pleased to see the tall lanky figure and long pale face of Henry George Parker, the only lawyer Wolfe would admit to the bar if he had the say. He came to shake my hand and said he'd have me out of there in a minute now.

"No rush," I said stiffly. "Don't let it interfere with anything important."

He laughed, haw-haw, and took me inside the gate. All the formalities but one which required my presence had already been attended to, and he made good on his minute. On the way up in the taxi he explained why I had been left to rot until past noon. Getting bail on the Sullivan Act charge had been simple, but I had also been tagged with a material witness warrant, and the DA had asked the judge to put it at fifty grand! He had been stubborn about it, and the best Parker could do was talk it down to twenty, and he had had to report back to Wolfe before closing the deal. I was not to leave the jurisdiction. As the taxi crossed Thirty-fourth Street I looked west across the river. I had never cared much for New Jersey, but now the idea of driving through the tunnel and on among the billboards seemed attractive.

I preceded Parker up the stoop at the old brownstone on West Thirty-fifth, used my key but found that the chain bolt was on, which was normal but not invariable when I was out of the house, and had to push the button. Fritz Brenner, chef and house manager, let us in and stood while we disposed of our coats and hats.

"Are you all right, Archie?" he inquired.

"No," I said frankly. "Don't you smell me?"

As we went down the hall Wolfe appeared, coming from the door to the dining room. He stopped and regarded me. I returned his gaze with my chin up.

"I'll go up and rinse off," I said, "while you're finishing lunch."

"I've finished," he said grimly. "Have you eaten?"

"Enough to hold me."

"Then we'll get started."

He marched into the office, across the hall from the dining room, went to his oversized chair behind his desk, sat, and got himself adjusted for comfort. Parker took the red leather chair. As I crossed to my desk I started talking, to get the jump on him.

"It will help," I said, not aggressively but pointedly, "if we first get it settled about my leaving that room with my gun there in the drawer. I do not—"

"Shut up!" Wolfe snapped.

"In that case," I demanded, "why didn't you leave me in the coop? I'll go back and—"

"Sit down!"

I sat.

"I deny," he said, "that you were in the slightest degree imprudent. Even if you were, this has transcended such petty considerations." He picked up a sheet of paper from his desk. "This is a letter which came yesterday from a Mrs. E. R. Baumgarten. She wants me to investigate the activities of a nephew who is employed by the business she owns. I wish to reply. Your notebook."

He was using what I call his conclusive tone, leaving no room for questions, let alone argument. I got my notebook and pen.

"Dear Mrs. Baumgarten." He went at it as if he had already composed it in his mind. "Thank you very much for your letter of the thirteenth, requesting me to undertake an investigation for you. Paragraph. I am sorry that I cannot be of service to you. I am compelled to decline because I have been informed by an official of the New York Police Department that my license to operate a private detective agency is about to be taken away from me. Sincerely yours."

Parker ejaculated something and got ignored. I stayed deadpan, but among my emotions was renewed regret that I had missed Wolfe's and Cramer's talk.

Wolfe was saying, "Type it at once and send Fritz to mail it. If any requests for appointments come by telephone refuse them, giving the reason and keeping a record."

"The reason given in the letter?"

"Yes."

I swiveled the typewriter to me, got paper and carbon in, and hit the keys. I had to concentrate. This was Cramer's farthest north. Parker was asking questions, and Wolfe was grunting at him. I finished the letter and envelope, had Wolfe sign it, went to the kitchen and told Fritz to take it to Eighth Avenue immediately, and returned to the office.

"Now," Wolfe said, "I want all of it. Go ahead."

Ordinarily when I start giving Wolfe a full report of an event, no matter how extended and involved, I just glide in and keep going with no effort at all, thanks to my long and hard training. That time, having just got a severe jolt, I wasn't so hot at the beginning, since I was supposed to include every word and movement, but by the time I had got to where I opened the window it was coming smooth and easy. As usual, Wolfe soaked it all in without making any interruptions.

It took all of an hour and a half, and then came questions, but not many. I rate a report by the number of questions he has when I'm through, and by that test this was up toward the top. Wolfe leaned back and closed his eyes.

Parker spoke. "It could have been any of them, but it must have been Koven. Or why his string of lies, knowing that you and Goodwin would both contradict him?" The lawyer haw-hawed. "That is, if they're lies—considering your settled policy of telling your counselor only what you think he should know."

"Pfui." Wolfe's eyes came open. "This is extraordinarily intricate, Archie. Have you examined it any?"

"I've started. When I pick at it, it gets worse instead of better."

"Yes. I'm afraid you'll have to type it out. By eleven tomorrow morning?"

"I guess so, but I need a bath first. Anyway, what for?

What can we do with it without a license? I suppose it's suspended?"

He ignored it. "What the devil is that smell?" he demanded.

"Disinfectant. It's for the bloodhounds in case you escape." I arose. "I'll go scrub."

"No." He glanced at the wall clock, which said 3:45—fifteen minutes to go until he was due to join Theodore and the orchids up on the roof. "An errand first. I believe it's the *Gazette* that carries the Dazzle Dan comic strip?"

"Yes, sir."

"Daily and Sunday?"

"Yes, sir."

"I want all of them for the past three years. Can you get them?"

"I can try."

"Do so."

"Now?"

"Yes. Wait a minute—confound it, don't be a cyclone! You should hear my instructions for Mr. Parker, but first one for you. Mail Mr. Koven a bill for recovery of his gun, five hundred dollars. It should go today."

"Any extras, under the circumstances?"

"No. Five hundred flat." Wolfe turned to the lawyer. "Mr. Parker, how long will it take to enter a suit for damages and serve a summons on the defendant?"

"That depends." Parker sounded like a lawyer. "If it's rushed all possible and there are no unforeseen obstacles and the defendant is accessible for service, it could be merely a matter of hours."

"By noon tomorrow?"

"Quite possibly, yes."

"Then proceed, please. Mr. Koven has destroyed, by slander, my means of livelihood. I wish to bring an action demanding payment by him of the sum of one million dollars."

"M-m-m-m," Parker said. He was frowning.

I addressed Wolfe. "I want to apologize," I told him, "for jumping to a conclusion. I was supposing you had lost control for once and buried it too deep in Cramer.

Whereas you did it purposely, getting set for this. I'll be damned."

Wolfe grunted.

"In this sort of thing," Parker said, "it is usual, and desirable, to first send a written request for recompense, by your attorney if you prefer. It looks better."

"I don't care how it looks. I want immediate action."

"Then we'll act." That was one of the reasons Wolfe stuck to Parker; he was no dilly-dallier. "But I must ask, isn't the sum a little flamboyant? A full million?"

"It is not flamboyant. At a hundred thousand a year, a modest expectation, my income would be a million in ten years. A detective license once lost in this fashion is not easily regained."

"All right. A million. I'll need all the facts for drafting a complaint."

"You have them. You've just heard Archie recount them. Must you stickle for more?"

"No. I'll manage." Parker got to his feet. "One thing, though, service of process may be a problem. Policemen may still be around, and even if they aren't I doubt if strangers will be getting into that house tomorrow."

"Archie will send Saul Panzer to you. Saul can get in anywhere and do anything." Wolfe wiggled a finger. "I want Mr. Koven to get that. I want to see him in this room. Five times this morning I tried to get him on the phone, without success. If that doesn't get him I'll devise something that will."

"He'll give it to his attorney."

"Then the attorney will come, and if he's not an imbecile I'll give myself thirty minutes to make him send for his client or go and get him. Well?"

Parker turned and left, not loitering. I got at the typewriter to make out a bill for half a grand, which seemed like a waste of paper after what I had just heard.

VI

AT MIDNIGHT that Tuesday the office was a sight. It has often been a mess, one way and another, including the time the strangled Cynthia Brown was lying on the floor with her tongue protruding, but this was something new. Dazzle Dan, both black-and-white and color, was all over the place. On account of our shortage in manpower, with me tied up on my typing job, Fritz and Theodore had been drafted for the chore of tearing out the pages and stacking them chronologically, ready for Wolfe to study. With Wolfe's permission, I had bribed Lon Cohen of the Gazette to have three years of Dazzle Dan assembled and delivered to us, by offering him an exclusive. Naturally he demanded specifications.

"Nothing much," I told him on the phone. "Only that Nero Wolfe is out of the detective business because Inspector Cramer is taking away his license."

"Quite a gag," Lon conceded.

"No gag. Straight."

"You mean it?"

"We're offering it for publication. Exclusive, unless Cramer's office spills it, and I don't think they will."

"The Getz murder?"

"Yes. Only a couple of paragraphs, because details are not yet available, even to you. I'm out on bail."

"I know you are. This is pie. We'll raid the files and get it over there as soon as we can."

He hung up without pressing for details. Of course that meant he would send Dazzle Dan COD, with a reporter. When the reporter arrived a couple of hours later, shortly after Wolfe had come down from the plant rooms at six o'clock, it wasn't just a man with a notebook, it was Lon Cohen himself. He came to the office with me, dumped a big heavy carton on the floor by my desk, removed his coat and dropped it on the carton to show that Dazzle Dan was his property until paid for, and demanded, "I want the works. What Wolfe said and what Cramer said. A picture of Wolfe studying Dazzle Dan—"

I pushed him into a chair, courteously, and gave him all we were ready to turn loose of. Naturally that wasn't enough; it never is. I let him fire questions up to a dozen or so, even answering one or two, and then made it clear that that was all for now and I had work to do. He admitted it was a bargain, stuck his notebook in his pocket, and got up and picked up his coat.

"If you're not in a hurry, Mr. Cohen," muttered Wolfe, who had left the interview to me.

Lon dropped the coat and sat down. "I have nineteen years, Mr. Wolfe. Before I retire."

"I won't detain you that long." Wolfe sighed. "I am no longer a detective, but I'm a primate and therefore curious. The function of a newspaperman is to satisfy curiosity. Who killed Mr. Getz?"

Lon's brows went up. "Archie Goodwin? It was his gun."

"Nonsense. I'm quite serious. Also I'm discreet. I am excluded from the customary sources of information by the jackassery of Mr. Cramer. I—"

"May I print that?"

"No. None of this. Nor shall I quote you. This is a private conversation. I would like to know what your colleagues are saying but not printing. Who killed Mr. Getz? Miss Lowell? If so, why?"

Lon pulled his lower lip down and let it up again. "You mean we're just talking."

"Yes."

"This might possibly lead to another talk that could be printed."

"It might. I make no commitment." Wolfe wasn't eager.

"You wouldn't. As for Miss Lowell, she has not been scratched. It is said that Getz learned she was chiseling on royalties from makers of Dazzle Dan products and intended to hang it on her. That could have been big money."

"Any names or dates?"

"None that are repeatable. By me. Yet."

"Any evidence?"

"I haven't seen any."

Wolfe grunted. "Mr. Hildebrand. If so, why?"

"That's shorter and sadder. He has told friends about it. He has been with Koven for eight years and was told last week he could leave at the end of the month, and he blamed it on Getz. He might or might not get another job at his age."

Wolfe nodded. "Mr. Jordan?"

Lon hesitated. "This I don't like, but others are talking, so why not us? They say Jordan has painted some pictures, modern stuff, and twice he has tried to get a gallery to show them, two different galleries, and both times Getz has somehow kiboshed it. This has names and dates, but whether because Getz was born a louse or whether he wanted to keep Jordan—"

"I'll do my own speculating, thank you. Mr. Getz may not have liked the pictures. Mr. Koven?"

Lon turned a hand over. "Well? What better could you ask? Getz had him buffaloed, no doubt about it. Getz ruled the roost, plenty of evidence on that, and nobody knows why, so the only question is what he had on Koven. It must have been good, but what was it? You say this is a private conversation?"

"Yes."

"Then here's something we got started on just this afternoon. It has to be checked before we print it. That house on Seventy-sixth Street is in Getz's name."

"Indeed." Wolfe shut his eyes and opened them again. "And Mrs. Koven?"

Lon turned his other hand over. "Husband and wife are one, aren't they?"

"Yes. Man and wife make one fool."

Lon's chin jerked up. "I want to print that. Why not?"

"It was printed more than three hundred years ago. Ben Jonson wrote it." Wolfe sighed. "Confound it, what can I do with only a few scraps?" He pointed at the carton. "You want that stuff back, I suppose?"

Lon said he did. He also said he would be glad to go on with the private conversation in the interest of justice and the public welfare, but apparently Wolfe had all the scraps he could use at the moment. After ushering Lon to the door I went up to my room to spend an hour attending to purely personal matters, a detail that had been too long postponed. I was out of the shower, selecting a shirt, when a call came from Saul Panzer in response to the message I had left. I gave him all the features of the picture that would help and told him to report to Parker's law office in the morning.

After dinner that evening we were all hard at it in the office. Fritz and Theodore were unfolding *Gazettes*, finding the right page and tearing it out, and carrying off the leavings. I was banging away at my machine, three pages an hour. Wolfe was at his desk, concentrating on a methodical and exhaustive study of three years of Dazzle Dan. It was well after midnight when he pushed back his chair, arose, stretched, rubbed his eyes, and told us, "It's bedtime. This morass of fatuity has given me indigestion. Good night."

Wednesday morning he tried to put one over. His routine was breakfast in his room, with the morning paper, at eight; then shaving and dressing; then, from nine to eleven, his morning shift up in the plant rooms. He never went to the office before eleven, and the detective business was never allowed to mingle with the orchids. But that Wednesday he fudged. While I was in the kitchen with Fritz, enjoying griddle cakes, Darst's sausage, honey, and plenty of coffee, and going through the morning papers, with two readings for the *Gazette's* account of Wolfe's enforced retirement, Wolfe sneaked downstairs into the office and made off with a stack of Dazzle Dan. The way I knew, before breakfast I had gone in there to straighten up a little, and I am trained to observe. Returning after breakfast, and glancing around before starting at my typewriter, I saw that half of a pile of Dan was gone. I don't think I had ever seen him quite so hot under the collar. I admit I fully approved. Not only did I not make an excuse for a trip up to the roof to catch him at it, but I even took the trouble to be out of the office when he came down at eleven o'clock, to give him a chance to get Dan back unseen.

My first job after breakfast had been to carry out some instructions Wolfe had given me the evening before. Manhattan office hours being what they are, I got no answer at the number of Levay Recorders, Inc., until 9:35. Then it took some talking to get a promise of immediate action, and if it hadn't been for the name of Nero Wolfe I wouldn't have made it. But I got both the promise and the action. A little after ten two men arrived with cartons of equipment and tool kits, and in less than an hour they were through and gone, and it was a neat and nifty job. It would have taken an expert search to reveal anything suspicious in the office, and the wire to the kitchen, running around the baseboard and on through, wouldn't be suspicious even if seen.

It was hard going at the typewriter on account of the phone ringing, chiefly reporters wanting to talk to Wolfe, or at least me, and finally I had to ask Fritz in to answer the damn thing and give everybody a brush-off. A call he switched to me was one from the DA's office. They had the nerve to ask me to come down there so they could ask me something. I told them I was busy answering Help Wanted ads and couldn't spare the time. Half an hour later Fritz switched another one to me. It was Sergeant Purley Stebbins. He was good and sore, beefing about Wolfe having no authority to break the news about losing his license, and it wasn't official yet, and where did I think it would get me refusing to cooperate with the DA on a murder when I had discovered the body, and I could have my choice of coming down quick or having a PD car come and get me. I let him use up his breath.

"Listen, brother," I told him, "I hadn't heard that the name of this city has been changed to Moscow. If Mr. Wolfe wants to publish it that he's out of business, hoping that someone will pass the hat or offer him a job as doorman, that's his affair. As for my cooperating, nuts. You have already got me sewed up on two charges, and on advice of counsel *and* my doctor I am staying home, taking

aspirin and gargling with prune juice and gin. If you come
here, no matter who, you won't get in without a search
warrant. If you come with another warrant for me, say for
cruelty to animals because I opened that window, you can
either wait on the stoop until I emerge or shoot the door
down, whichever you prefer. I am now hanging up."

"If you'll listen a minute, damn it."

"Good-by, you double-breasted nitwit."

I cradled the phone, sat thirty seconds to calm down,
and resumed at the typewriter. The next interruption
came not from the outside but from Wolfe, a little before
noon. He was back at his desk, analyzing Dazzle Dan.
Suddenly he pronounced my name, and I swiveled.

"Yes, sir."

"Look at this."

He slid a sheet of the *Gazette* across his desk, and I got
up and took it. It was a Sunday half-page, in color, from
four months back. In the first frame Dazzle Dan was
scooting along a country road on a motorcycle, passing a
roadside sign that read:

PEACHES RIGHT FROM THE TREE!
AGGIE GHOOL AND HAGGIE KROOL

Frame two, D.D. had stopped his bike alongside a peach
tree full of red and yellow fruit. Standing there were two
females, presumably Aggie Ghool and Haggie Krool. One
was old and bent, dressed in burlap as near as I could tell;
the other was young and pink-cheeked, wearing a mink
coat. If you say surely not a mink coat, I say I'm telling
what I saw. D.D. was saying, in his balloon, "Gimme a
dozen."

Frame three, the young female was handing D.D. the
peaches, and the old one was extending her hand for payment. Frame four, the old one was giving D.D. his change
from a bill. Frame five, the old one was handing the young
one a coin and saying, "Here's your ten per cent, Haggie,"
and the young one was saying, "Thank you very much,
Aggie." Frame six, D.D. was asking Aggie, "Why don't
you split it even?" and Aggie was telling him, "Because it's

my tree." Frame seven, D.D. was off again on the bike, but I felt I had had enough and looked at Wolfe inquiringly.

"Am I supposed to comment?"

"If it would help, yes."

"I pass. If it's a feed from the National Industrialists' League it's the wrong angle. If you mean the mink coat, Pat Lowell's may not be paid for."

He grunted. "There have been two similar episodes, one each year, with the same characters."

"Then it may be paid for."

"Is that all?"

"It's all for now. I'm not a brain, I'm a typist. I've got to finish this damn report."

I tossed the art back to him and returned to work.

At 12:28 I handed him the finished report, and he dropped D.D. and started on it. I went to the kitchen to tell Fritz I would take on the phone again, and as I re-entered the office it was ringing. I crossed to my desk and got it. My daytime formula was, "Nero Wolfe's office, Archie Goodwin speaking," but with our license gone it was presumably illegal to have an office, so I said, "Nero Wolfe's residence, Archie Goodwin speaking," and heard Saul Panzer's husky voice.

"Reporting in, Archie. No trouble at all. Koven is served. Put it in his hand five minutes ago."

"In the house?"

"Yes. I'll call Parker—"

"How did you get in?"

"Oh, simple. The man that delivers stuff from that Furnari's you told me about has got the itch bad, and it only took ten bucks. Of course after I got inside I had to use my head and legs both, but with your sketch of the layout it was a cinch."

"For you, yes. Mr. Wolfe says satisfactory, which as you know is as far as he ever goes. I say you show promise. You'll call Parker?"

"Yes. I have to go there to sign a paper."

"Okay. Be seeing you."

I hung up and told Wolfe. He lifted his eyes, said, "Ah!" and returned to the report.

After lunch there was an important chore, involving Wolfe, me, our memory of the talk Saturday evening with Koven, and the equipment that had been installed by Levay Recorders, Inc. We spent nearly an hour at it, with three separate tries, before we got it done to Wolfe's satisfaction.

After that it dragged along, at least for me. The phone calls had fallen off. Wolfe, at his desk, finished with the report, put it in a drawer, leaned back, and closed his eyes. I would just as soon have opened a conversation, but pretty soon his lips started working—pushing out, drawing back, and pushing out again—and I knew his brain was busy so I went to the cabinet for a batch of the germination records and settled down to making entries. He didn't need a license to go on growing orchids, though the question would soon arise of how to pay the bills. At four o'clock he left to go up to the plant rooms, and I went on with the records. During the next two hours there were a few phone calls, but none from Koven or his lawyer or Parker. At two minutes past six I was telling myself that Koven was probably drinking himself up to something, no telling what, when two things happened at once: the sound came from the hall of Wolfe's elevator jerking to a stop, and the doorbell rang.

I went to the hall, switched on the stoop light, and took a look through the panel of one-way glass in the front door. It was a mink coat all right, but the hat was different. I went closer, passing Wolfe on his way to the office, got a view of the face, and saw that she was alone. I marched to the office door and announced, "Miss Patricia Lowell. Will she do?"

He made a face. He seldom welcomes a man crossing his threshold; he never welcomes a woman. "Let her in," he muttered.

I stepped to the front, slid the bolt off, and opened up. "This is the kind of surprise I like," I said heartily. She entered, and I shut the door and bolted it. "Couldn't you find a coconut?"

"I want to see Nero Wolfe," she said in a voice so hard

that it was out of character, considering her pink cheeks.

"Sure. This way." I ushered her down the hall and on in. Once in a while Wolfe rises when a woman enters his office, but this time he kept not only his chair but also his tongue. He inclined his head a quarter of an inch when I pronounced her name, but said nothing. I gave her the red leather chair, helped her throw her coat back, and went to my desk.

"So you're Nero Wolfe," she said.

That called for no comment and got none.

"I'm scared to death," she said.

"You don't look it," Wolfe growled.

"I hope I don't; I'm trying not to." She started to put her bag on the little table at her elbow, changed her mind, and kept it in her lap. She took off a glove. "I was sent here by Mr. Koven."

No comment. We were looking at her. She looked at me, then back at Wolfe, and protested, "My God, don't you ever say anything?"

"Only on occasion." Wolfe leaned back. "Give me one. You say something."

She compressed her lips. She was sitting forward and erect in the big roomy chair, with no contact with the upholstered back. "Mr. Koven sent me," she said, clipping it, "about the ridiculous suit for damages you have brought. He intends to enter a counterclaim for damage to his reputation through actions of your acknowledged agent, Archie Goodwin. Of course he denies that there is any basis for your suit."

She stopped. Wolfe met her gaze and kept his trap shut.

"That's the situation," she said belligerently.

"Thank you for coming to tell me," Wolfe murmured. "If you'll show Miss Lowell the way out, please, Archie?"

I stood up. She looked at me as if I had offered her a deadly insult, and looked back at Wolfe. "I don't think," she said, "that your attitude is very sensible. I think you and Mr. Koven should come to an agreement on this. Why wouldn't this be the way to do it—say the claims cancel each other, and you abandon yours and he abandons his?"

"Because," Wolfe said dryly, "my claim is valid and his isn't. If you're a member of the bar, Miss Lowell, you should know that this is a little improper, or anyway unconventional. You should be talking with my attorney, not with me."

"I'm not a lawyer, Mr. Wolfe. I'm Mr. Koven's agent and business manager. He thinks lawyers would just make this more of a mess than it is, and I agree with him. He thinks you and he should settle it between you. Isn't that possible?"

"I don't know. We can try. There's a phone. Get him down here."

She shook her head. "He's not—he's too upset. I'm sure you'll find it more practical to deal with me, and if we come to an understanding he'll approve, I guarantee that. Why don't we go into it—the two claims?"

"I doubt if it will get us anywhere." Wolfe sounded perfectly willing to come halfway. "For one thing, a factor in both claims is the question who killed Adrian Getz and why? If it was Mr. Goodwin, Mr. Koven's claim has a footing, and I freely concede it; if it was someone else I concede nothing. If I discussed it with you I would have to begin by considering that aspect; I would have to ask you some pointed questions; and I doubt if you would dare to risk answering them."

"I can always button up. What kind of questions?"

"Well—" Wolfe pursed his lips. "For example, how's the monkey?"

"I can risk answering that. It's sick. It's at the Speyer Hospital. They don't expect it to live."

"Exposure from the open window?"

"Yes. They're very delicate, that kind."

Wolfe nodded. "That table over there by the globe—that pile of stuff on it is Dazzle Dan for the past three years. I've been looking through it. Last August and September a monkey had a prominent role. It was drawn by two different persons, or at least with two different conceptions. In its first seventeen appearances it was depicted maliciously—on a conjecture, by someone with a distaste for monkeys. Thereafter it was drawn sympathetically and humorously. The change was abrupt and noticeable. Why? On instructions from Mr. Koven?"

Pat Lowell was frowning. Her lips parted and went together again.

"You have four choices," Wolfe said bluntly. "The truth, a lie, evasion, or refusal to answer. Either of the last two would make me curious, and I would get my curiosity satisfied somehow. If you try a lie it may work, but I'm an expert on lies and liars."

"There's nothing to lie about. I was thinking back. Mr. Getz objected to the way the monkey was drawn, and Mr. Koven had Mr. Jordan do it instead of Mr. Hildebrand."

"Mr. Jordan likes monkeys?"

"He likes animals. He said the monkey looked like Napoleon."

"Mr. Hildebrand does not like monkeys?"

"He didn't like that one. Rookaloo knew it, of course, and bit him once. Isn't this pretty silly, Mr. Wolfe? Are you going on with this?"

"Unless you walk out, yes. I'm investigating Mr. Koven's counterclaim, and this is how I do it. With any question you have your four choices—and a fifth too, of course: get up and go. How did you feel about the monkey?"

"I thought it was an awful nuisance, but it had its points as a diversion. It was my fault it was there, since I gave it to Mr. Getz."

"Indeed. When?"

"About a year ago. A friend returning from South America gave it to me, and I couldn't take care of it so I gave it to him."

"Mr. Getz lives at the Koven house?"

"Yes."

"Then actually you were dumping it onto Mrs. Koven. Did she appreciate it?"

"She has never said so. I didn't—I know I should have considered that. I apologized to her, and she was nice about it."

"Did Mr. Koven like the monkey?"

"He liked to tease it. But he didn't dislike it; he teased it just to annoy Mr. Getz."

Wolfe leaned back and clasped his hands behind his head. "You know, Miss Lowell, I did not find the Dazzle Dan saga hopelessly inane. There is a sustained sardonic tone, some fertility of invention, and even an occasional touch of imagination. Monday evening, while Mr. Goodwin was in jail, I telephoned a couple of people who are supposed to know things and was referred by them to others. I was told that it is generally believed, though not published, that the conception of Dazzle Dan was originally supplied to Mr. Koven by Mr. Getz, that Mr. Getz was the continuing source of inspiration for the story and pictures, and that without him Mr. Koven will be up a stump. What about it?"

Pat Lowell had stiffened. "Talk." She was scornful. "Just cheap talk."

"You should know." Wolfe sounded relieved. "If that belief could be validated I admit I would be up a stump myself. To support my claim against Mr. Koven, and to discredit his against me, I need to demonstrate that Mr. Goodwin did not kill Mr. Getz, either accidentally or otherwise. If he didn't, then who did? One of you five. But all of you had a direct personal interest in the continued success of Dazzle Dan, sharing as you did in the prodigious proceeds; and if Mr. Getz was responsible for the success, why kill him?" Wolfe chuckled. "So you see I'm not silly at all. We've been at it only twenty minutes, and already you've helped me enormously. Give us another four or five hours, and we'll see. By the way."

He leaned forward to press a button at the edge of his desk, and in a moment Fritz appeared.

"There'll be a guest for dinner, Fritz."

"Yes, sir." Fritz went.

"Four or five hours?" Pat Lowell demanded.

"At least that. With a recess for dinner; I banish business from the table. Half for me and half for you. This affair is extremely complicated, and if you came here to get an agreement we'll have to cover it all. Let's see, where were we?"

She regarded him. "About Getz, I didn't say he had

nothing to do with the success of Dazzle Dan. After all, so do I. I didn't say he won't be a loss. Everyone knows he was Mr. Koven's oldest and closest friend. We were all quite aware that Mr. Koven relied on him—"

Wolfe showed her a palm. "Please, Miss Lowell, don't spoil it for me. Don't give me a point and then try to snatch it back. Next you'll be saying that Koven called Getz 'the Squirt' to show his affection, as a man will call his dearest friend an old bastard, whereas I prefer to regard it as an inferiority complex, deeply resentful, showing its biceps. Or telling me that all of you, without exception, were inordinately fond of Mr. Getz and submissively grateful to him. Don't forget that Mr. Goodwin spent hours in that house among you and has fully reported to me; also you should know that I had a talk with Inspector Cramer Monday evening and learned from him some of the plain facts, such as the pillow lying on the floor, scorched and pierced, showing that it had been used to muffle the sound of the shot, and the failure of all of you to prove lack of opportunity."

Wolfe kept going. "But if you insist on minimizing Koven's dependence as a fact, let me assume it as a hypothesis in order to put a question. Say, just for my question, that Koven felt strongly about his debt to Getz and his reliance on him, that he proposed to do something about it, and that he found it necessary to confide in one of you people, to get help or advice. Which of you would he have come to? We must of course put his wife first, ex officio and to sustain convention—and anyway, out of courtesy I must suppose you incapable of revealing your employer's conjugal privities. Which of you three would he have come to—Mr. Hildebrand, Mr. Jordan, or you?"

Miss Lowell was wary. "On your hypothesis, you mean."

"Yes."

"None of us."

"But if he felt he had to?"

"Not with anything as intimate as that. He wouldn't have let himself have to. None of us three has ever got within miles of him on anything really personal."

"Surely he confides in you, his agent and manager?"

"On business matters, yes. Not on personal things, except superficialities."

"Why were all of you so concerned about the gun in his desk?"

"We weren't concerned, not *really* concerned—at least I wasn't. I just didn't like it's being there, loaded, so easy to get at, and I knew he didn't have a license for it."

Wolfe kept on about the gun for a good ten minutes—how often had she seen it, had she ever picked it up, and so forth, with special emphasis on Sunday morning, when she and Hildebrand had opened the drawer and looked at it. On that detail she corroborated Hildebrand as I had heard him tell it to Cramer. Finally she balked. She said they weren't getting anywhere, and she certainly wasn't going to stay for dinner if afterward it was only going to be more of the same.

Wolfe nodded in agreement. "You're quite right," he told her. "We've gone as far as we can, you and I. We need all of them. It's time for you to call Mr. Koven and tell him so. Tell him to be here at eight-thirty with Mrs. Koven, Mr. Jordan, and Mr. Hildebrand."

She was staring at him. "Are you trying to be funny?" she demanded.

He skipped it. "I don't know," he said, "whether you can handle it properly; if not, I'll talk to him. The validity of my claim, and of his, depends primarily on who killed Mr. Getz. I now know who killed him. I'll have to tell the police but first I want to settle the matter of my claim with Mr. Koven. Tell him that. Tell him that if I have to inform the police before I have a talk with him and the others there will be no compromise on my claim, and I'll collect it."

"This is a bluff."

"Then call it."

"I'm going to." She left the chair and got the coat around her. Her eyes blazed at him. "I'm not such a sap!" She started for the door.

"Get Inspector Cramer, Archie!" Wolfe snapped. He called, "They'll be there by the time you are!"

I lifted the phone and dialed. She was out in the hall, but I heard neither footsteps nor the door opening.

"Hello," I told the transmitter, loud enough. "Manhattan Homicide West? Inspector Cramer, please. This is—"

A hand darted past me, and a finger pressed the button down, and a mink coat dropped to the floor. "Damn you!" she said, hard and cold, but the hand was shaking so that the finger slipped off the button. I cradled the phone.

"Get Mr. Koven's number for her, Archie," Wolfe purred.

VII

A T TWENTY minutes to nine Wolfe's eyes moved slowly from left to right, to take in the faces of our assembled visitors. He was in a nasty humor. He hated to work right after dinner, and from the way he kept his chin down and a slight twitch of a muscle in his cheek I knew it was going to be real work. Whether he had got them there with a bluff or not, and my guess was that he had, it would take more than a bluff to rake in the pot he was after now.

Pat Lowell had not dined with us. Not only had she declined to come along to the dining room; she had also left untouched the tray which Fritz had taken to her in the office. Of course that got Wolfe's goat and probably got some pointed remarks from him, but I wasn't there to hear them because I had gone to the kitchen to check with Fritz on the operation of the installation that had been made by Levay Recorders, Inc. That was the one part of the program that I clearly understood. I was still in the kitchen, rehearsing with Fritz, when the doorbell rang and I went to the front and found them there in a body. They got better hall service than I had got at their place, and also better chair service in the office.

When they were seated Wolfe took them in from left to right—Harry Koven in the red leather chair, then his wife, then Pat Lowell, and, after a gap, Pete Jordan and Byram Hildebrand over toward me. I don't know what impression Wolfe got from his survey, but from where I sat it looked as if he was up against a united front.

"This time," Koven blurted, "you can't cook up a fancy lie with Goodwin. There are witnesses."

He was keyed up. I would have said he had had six drinks, but it might have been more.

"We won't get anywhere that way, Mr. Koven," Wolfe objected. "We're all tangled up, and it will take more than blather to get us loose. You don't want to pay me a million dollars. I don't want to lose my license. The police don't want to add another unsolved murder to the long list. The central and dominant factor is the violent death of Mr. Getz, and I propose to deal with that at length. If we can get that settled—"

"You told Miss Lowell you know who killed him. If so, why don't you tell the police? That ought to settle it."

Wolfe's eyes narrowed. "You don't mean that, Mr. Koven—"

"You're damn right I mean it!"

"Then there's a misunderstanding. I heard Miss Lowell's talk with you on the phone, both ends of it. I got the impression that my threat to inform the police about Mr. Getz's death was what brought you down here. Now you seem—"

"It wasn't any threat that brought me here! It's that blackmailing suit you started! I want to make you eat it and I'm going to!"

"Indeed. Then I gather that you don't care who gets my information first, you or the police. But I do. For one thing, when I talk to the police I like to be able—"

The doorbell rang. When visitors were present Fritz usually answered the door, but he had orders to stick to his post in the kitchen, so I got up and went to the hall, circling behind the arc of the chairs. I switched on the stoop light for a look through the one-way glass. One glance was enough. Stepping back into the office, I stood until Wolfe caught my eye.

"The man about the chair," I told him.

He frowned. "Tell him I'm—" He stopped, and the

frown cleared. "No. I'll see him. If you'll excuse me a moment?" He pushed his chair back, made it to his feet, and came, detouring around Koven. I let him precede me into the hall and closed that door before joining him. He strode to the front, peered through the glass, and opened the door. The chain bolt stopped it at a crack of two inches.

Wolfe spoke through the crack. "Well, sir?"

Inspector Cramer's voice was anything but friendly. "I'm coming in."

"I doubt it. What for?"

"Patricia Lowell entered here at six o'clock and is still here. The other four entered fifteen minutes ago. I told you Monday evening to lay off. I told you your license was suspended, and here you are with your office full. I'm coming in."

"I still doubt it. I have no client. My job for Mr. Koven, which you know about, has been finished, and I have sent him a bill. These people are here to discuss an action for damages which I have brought against Mr. Koven. I don't need a license for that. I'm shutting the door."

He tried to, but it didn't budge. I could see the tip of Cramer's toe at the bottom of the crack.

"By God, this does it," Cramer said savagely. "You're through."

"I thought I was already through. But this—"

"I can't hear you! The wind."

"This is preposterous, talking through a crack. Descend to the sidewalk, and I'll come out. Did you hear that?"

"Yes."

"Very well. To the sidewalk."

Wolfe marched to the big old walnut rack and reached for his overcoat. After I had held it for him and handed him his hat I got my coat and slipped into it and then took a look through the glass. The stoop was empty. A burly figure was at the bottom of the steps. I unbolted the door and opened it, followed Wolfe over the sill, pulled the door shut, and made sure it was locked. A gust of wind pounced on us, slashing at us with sleet. I wanted to take Wolfe's elbow as we went down the steps, thinking where it would leave me if he fell and cracked his skull, but knew I hadn't better.

He made it safely, got his back to the sleety wind, which meant that Cramer had to face it, and raised his voice. "I don't like fighting a blizzard, so let's get to the point. You don't want these people talking with me, but there's nothing you can do about it. You have blundered and you know it. You arrested Mr. Goodwin on a trumpery charge. You came and blustered me and went too far. Now you're afraid I'm going to explode Mr. Koven's lies. More, you're afraid I'm going to catch a murderer and toss him to the district attorney. So you—"

"I'm not afraid of a goddam thing." Cramer was squinting to protect his eyes from the cutting sleet. "I told you to lay off, and by God you're going to. Your suit against Koven is a phony."

"It isn't, but let's stick to the point. I'm uncomfortable. I am not an outdoors man. You want to enter my house. You may, under a condition. The five callers are in my office. There is a hole in the wall, concealed from view in the office by what is apparently a picture. Standing, or on a stool, in a nook at the end of the hall, you can see and hear us in the office. The condition is that you enter quietly —confound it!"

The wind had taken his hat. I made a quick dive and stab but missed, and away it went. He had only had it fourteen years.

"The condition," he repeated, "is that you enter quietly, take your post in the nook, oversee us from there, and give me half an hour. Thereafter you will be free to join us if you think you should. I warn you not to be impetuous. Up to a certain point your presence would make it harder for me, if not impossible, and I doubt if you'll know when that point is reached. I'm after a murderer, and there's one chance in five, I should say, that I'll get him. I want—"

"I thought you said you were discussing an action for damages."

"We are. I'll get either the murderer or the damages. Do you want to harp on that?"

"No."

"You've cooled off, and no wonder, in this hurricane. My hair will go next. I'm going in. If you come along it must be under the condition as stated. Are you coming?"

"Yes."

"You accept the condition?"

"Yes."

Wolfe headed for the steps. I passed him to go ahead and unlock the door. When they were inside I closed it and put the bolt back on. They hung up their coats, and Wolfe took Cramer down the hall and around the corner to the nook. I brought a stool from the kitchen, but Cramer shook his head. Wolfe slid the panel aside, making no sound, looked through, and nodded to Cramer. Cramer took a look and nodded back, and we left him. At the door to the office Wolfe muttered about his hair, and I let him use my pocket comb.

From the way they looked at us as we entered you might have thought they suspected we had been in the cellar fusing a bomb, but one more suspicion wouldn't make it any harder. I circled to my desk and sat. Wolfe got himself back in place, took a deep breath, and passed his eyes over them.

"I'm sorry," he said politely, "but that was unavoidable. Suppose we start over"—he looked at Koven—"say with your surmise to the police that Getz was shot by Mr. Goodwin accidentally in a scuffle. That's absurd. Getz was shot with a cartridge that had been taken from your gun and put into Goodwin's gun. Manifestly Goodwin couldn't have done that, since when he first saw your gun Getz was already dead. Therefore—"

"That's not true!" Koven cut in. "He had seen it before, when he came to my office. He could have gone back later and got the cartridges."

Wolfe glared at him in astonishment. "Do you really dare, sir, in front of me, to my face, to cling to that fantastic tale you told the police? That rigmarole?"

"You're damn right I do!"

"Pfui." Wolfe was disgusted. "I had hoped, here together, we were prepared to get down to reality. It would have been better to adopt your suggestion to take my information to the police. Perhaps—"

"I made no such suggestion!"

"In this room, Mr. Koven, some fifteen minutes ago?"

"No!"

Wolfe made a face. "I see," he said quietly. "It's impossible to get on solid ground with a man like you, but I still have to try. Archie, bring the tape from the kitchen, please?"

I went. I didn't like it. I thought he was rushing it. Granting that he had been jostled off his stride by Cramer's arrival, I felt that it was far from one of his best performances, and this looked like a situation where nothing less than his best would do. So I went to the kitchen, passing Cramer in his nook without a glance, told Fritz to stop the machine and wind, and stood and scowled at it turning. When it stopped I removed the wheel and slipped it into a carton and, carton in hand, returned to the office.

"We're waiting," Wolfe said curtly.

That hurried me. There was a stack of similar cartons on my desk, and in my haste I knocked them over as I was putting down the one I had brought. It was embarrassing with all eyes on me, and I gave them a cold look as I crossed to the cabinet to get the player. It needed a whole corner of my desk, and I had to shove the tumbled cartons aside to make room. Finally I had the player in position and connected, and the wheel of tape, taken from the carton, in place.

"All right?" I asked Wolfe.

"Go ahead."

I flipped the switch. There was a crackle and a little spitting, and then Wolfe's voice came:

"*It's not that, Mr. Koven, not at all. I only doubt if it's worth it to you, considering the size of my minimum fee, to hire me for anything so trivial as finding a stolen gun, or even discovering the thief. I should think—*"

"No!" Wolfe bellowed.

I switched it off. I was flustered. "Excuse it," I said. "The wrong one."

"Must I do it myself?" Wolfe asked sarcastically.

I muttered something, turning the wheel to rewind. I removed it, pawed among the cartons, picked one, took out the wheel, put it on, and turned the switch. This time the voice that came on was not Wolfe's but Koven's—loud and clear.

"*This time you can't cook up a fancy lie with Goodwin. There are witnesses.*"

Then Wolfe's: "*We won't get anywhere that way, Mr. Koven. We're all tangled up, and it will take more than blather to get us loose. You don't want to pay me a million dollars. I don't want to lose my license. The police don't want to add another unsolved murder to the long list. The central and dominant factor is the violent death of Mr. Getz, and I propose to deal with that at length. If we can get that settled—*"

Koven's: "*You told Miss Lowell you know who killed him. If so, why don't you tell the police? That ought to settle it.*"

Wolfe: "*You don't mean that, Mr. Koven—*"

Koven: "*You're damn right I mean it!*"

Wolfe: "*Then there's a misunderstanding. I heard Miss Lowell's talk with you on the phone, both ends of it. I got the impression that my threat to inform the police—*"

"That's enough!" Wolfe called. I turned it off. Wolfe looked at Koven. "I would call that," he said dryly, "a suggestion that I take my information to the police. Wouldn't you?"

Koven wasn't saying. Wolfe's eyes moved. "Wouldn't you, Miss Lowell?"

She shook her head. "I'm not an expert on suggestions."

Wolfe left her. "We won't quarrel over terms, Mr. Koven. You heard it. Incidentally, about the other tape you heard the start of through Mr. Goodwin's clumsiness, you may wonder why I haven't given it to the police to refute you. Monday evening, when Inspector Cramer came to see me, I still considered you as my client and I didn't want to discomfit you until I heard what you had to say. Before Mr. Cramer left he had made himself so offensive that I was disinclined to tell him anything whatever. Now you are no longer my client. We'll discuss this matter realistically or not at all. I don't care to badger you into an explicit statement that you lied to the police; I'll leave that to you and them; I merely insist that we proceed on the basis of what we both know to be the truth. With that understood—"

"Wait a minute," Pat Lowell put in. "The gun was in the drawer Sunday morning. I saw it."

"I know you did. That's one of the knots in the tangle, and we'll come to it." His eyes swept the arc. "We want to know who killed Adrian Getz. Let's get at it. What do we know about him or her? We know a lot.

"First, he took Koven's gun from the drawer sometime previous to last Friday and kept it somewhere. For that gun was put back in the drawer when Goodwin's was removed shortly before Getz was killed, and cartridges from it were placed in Goodwin's gun.

"Second, the thought of Getz continuing to live was for some reason so repugnant to him as to be intolerable.

"Third, he knew the purpose of Koven's visit here Saturday evening, and of Goodwin's errand at the Koven house on Monday, and he knew the details of the procedure planned by Koven and Goodwin. Only with—"

"I don't know them even yet," Hildebrand squeaked.

"Neither do I," Pete Jordan declared.

"The innocent can afford ignorance," Wolfe told them. "Enjoy it if you have it. Only with that knowledge could he have devised his intricate scheme and carried it out.

"Fourth, his mental processes are devious but defective. His deliberate and spectacular plan to make it appear that Goodwin had killed Getz, while ingenious in some respects, was in others witless. Going to Koven's office to get Goodwin's gun from the drawer and placing Koven's gun there, transferring the cartridges from Koven's gun to Goodwin's, proceeding to the room below to find Getz asleep, shooting him in the head, using a pillow to muffle the sound—all that was well enough, competently conceived and daringly executed, but then what? Wanting to make sure that the gun would be quickly found on the spot, a quite unnecessary precaution, he slipped it into the monkey's cage. That was probably improvisation and utterly brainless. Mr. Goodwin couldn't possibly be such a vapid fool.

"Fifth, he hated the monkey deeply and bitterly, either on its own account or because of its association with Getz. Having just killed a man, and needing to leave the spot with all possible speed, he went and opened a window, from only one conceivable motive. That took a peculiar, indeed an unexampled, malevolence. I admit it was effective. Miss Lowell tells me the monkey is dying.

"Sixth, he placed Koven's gun in the drawer Sunday morning and, after it had been seen there, took it out again. That was the most remarkable stratagem of all. Since there was no point in putting it there unless it was to be seen, he arranged that it should be seen. Why? It could only have been that he already knew what was to happen on Monday when Mr. Goodwin came, he had already conceived his scheme for framing Goodwin for the homicide, and he thought he was arranging in advance to discredit Goodwin's story. So he not only put the gun in the drawer Sunday morning, he also made sure its presence would be noted—and not, of course, by Mr. Koven."

Wolfe focused on one of them. "You saw the gun in the drawer Sunday morning, Mr. Hildebrand?"

"Yes." The squeak was off pitch. "But I didn't put it there!"

"I didn't say you did. Your claim to innocence has not yet been challenged. You were in the workroom, went up to consult Mr. Koven, encountered Mrs. Koven one flight up, were told by her that Mr. Koven was still in bed, ascended to the office, found Miss Lowell there, and you pulled the drawer open and both of you saw the gun there. Is that correct?"

"I didn't go up there to look in that drawer. We just—"

"Stop meeting accusations that haven't been made. It's a bad habit. Had you been upstairs earlier that morning?"

"No!"

"Had he, Miss Lowell?"

"Not that I know of." She spoke slowly, with a drag, as

if she had only so many words and had to count them. "Our looking into the drawer was only incidental."

"Had he, Mrs. Koven?"

The wife jerked her head up. "Had what?" she demanded.

"Had Mr. Hildebrand been upstairs earlier that morning?"

She looked bewildered. "Earlier than what?"

"You met him in the second-floor hall and told him that your husband was still in bed and that Miss Lowell was up in the office. Had he been upstairs before that? That morning?"

"I haven't the slightest idea."

"Then you don't say that he had been?"

"I know nothing about it."

"There's nothing as safe as ignorance—or as dangerous." Wolfe spread his gaze again. "To complete the list of what we know about the murderer. Seventh and last, his repugnance to Getz was so extreme that he even scorned the risk that by killing Getz he might be killing Dazzle Dan. How essential Getz was to Dazzle Dan—"

"*I* make Dazzle Dan!" Harry Koven roared. "Dazzle Dan is mine!" He was glaring at everybody. "*I* am Dazzle Dan!"

"For God's sake shut up, Harry!" Pat Lowell said sharply.

Koven's chin was quivering. He needed three drinks.

"I was saying," Wolfe went on, "that I do not know how essential Getz was to Dazzle Dan. The testimony conflicts. In any case the murderer wanted him dead. I've identified the murderer for you by now, surely?"

"You have not," Pat Lowell said aggressively.

"Then I'll specify." Wolfe leaned forward at them. "But first let me say a word for the police, particularly Mr. Cramer. He is quite capable of unraveling a tangle like this, with its superficial complexities. What flummoxed him was Mr. Koven's elaborate lie, apparently corroborated by Miss Lowell and Mr. Hildebrand. If he had had the gumption to proceed on the assumption that Mr. Goodwin and I were telling the truth and all of it, he would have found it simple. This should be a lesson to him."

Wolfe considered a moment. "It might be better to specify by elimination. If you recall my list of seven facts about the murderer, that is child's play. Mr. Jordan, for instance, is eliminated by Number Six; he wasn't there Sunday morning. Mr. Hildebrand is eliminated by three or four of them, especially Number Six again; he had made no earlier trip upstairs. Miss Lowell is eliminated, for me, by Numbers Four and Five; and I am convinced that none of the three I have named can meet the requirements of Number Three. I do not believe that Mr. Koven would have confided in any of them so intimately. Nor do I—"

"Hold it!" The gruff voice came from the doorway.

Heads jerked around. Cramer advanced and stopped at Koven's left, between him and his wife. There was dead silence. Koven had his neck twisted to stare up at Cramer, then suddenly he fell apart and buried his face in his hands.

Cramer, scowling at Wolfe, boiling with rage, spoke. "Damn you, if you had given it to us! You and your numbers game!"

"I can't give you what you won't take," Wolfe said bitingly. "You can have her now. Do you want more help? Mr. Koven was still in bed Sunday morning when two of them saw the gun in the drawer. More? Spend the night with Mr. Hildebrand. I'll stake my license against your badge that he'll remember that when he spoke with Mrs. Koven in the hall she said something that caused him to open the drawer and look at the gun. Still more? Take all the contents of her room to your laboratory. She must have hid the gun among her intimate things, and you should find evidence. You can't put him on the stand and ask him if and when he told her what he was doing; he can't testify against his wife; but surely—"

Mrs. Koven stood up. She was pale but under control, perfectly steady. She looked down at the back of her husband's bent head.

"Take me home, Harry," she said.

Cramer, in one short step, was at her elbow.

"Harry!" she said, softly insistent. "Take me home."

His head lifted and turned to look at her. I couldn't see his face. "Sit down, Marcy," he said. "I'll handle this." He looked at Wolfe. "If you've got a record of what I said here Saturday, all right. I lied to the cops. So what? I didn't want—"

"Be quiet, Harry," Pat Lowell blurted at him. "Get a lawyer and let him talk. Don't say anything."

Wolfe nodded. "That's good advice. Especially, Mr. Koven, since I hadn't quite finished. It is a matter of record that Mr. Getz not only owned the house you live in but also that he owned Dazzle Dan and permitted you to take only ten per cent of the proceeds."

Mrs. Koven dropped back into the chair and froze, staring at him. Wolfe spoke to her. "I suppose, madam, that after you killed him you went to his room to look for documents and possibly found some and destroyed them. That must have been part of your plan last week when you first took the gun from the drawer—to destroy all evidence of his ownership of Dazzle Dan after killing him. That was foolish, since a man like Mr. Getz would surely not leave invaluable papers in so accessible a spot, and they will certainly be found; we can leave that to Mr. Cramer. When I said it is a matter of record I meant a record that I have inspected and have in my possession."

Wolfe pointed. "That stack of stuff on that table is Dazzle Dan for the past three years. In one episode, repeated annually with variations, he buys peaches from two characters named Aggie Ghool and Haggie Krool, and Aggie Ghool, saying that she owns the tree, gives Haggie Krool ten per cent of the amount received and pockets the rest. A.G. are the initials of Adrian Getz; H.K. are the initials of Harry Koven. It is not credible that that is coincidence or merely a prank, especially since the episode was repeated annually. Mr. Getz must have had a singularly contorted psyche, taking delight as he did in hiding the fact of his ownership and control of that monster, but compelling the nominal owner to publish it each year in a childish allegory. For a meager ten per cent—"

"Not of the net," Koven objected. "Ten per cent of the gross. Over four hundred a week clear, and I—"

He stopped. His wife had said, "You worm." Leaving

her chair, she stood looking down at him, stiff and towering, overwhelming, small as she was.

"You worm!" she said in bitter contempt. "Not even a
worm. Worms have guts, don't they?"

She whirled to face Wolfe. "All right, you've got him.
The one time he ever acted like a man, and he didn't have
the guts to see it through. Getz owned Dazzle Dan, that's
right. When he got the idea and sold it, years ago, and
took Harry in to draw it and front it, Harry should have
insisted on an even split right then and didn't. He never
had it in him to insist on anything, and never would, and
Getz knew it. When Dazzle Dan caught on, and the years
went by and it kept getting bigger and bigger, Getz didn't
mind Harry having the name and the fame as long as he
owned it and got the money. You said he had a contorted
psyche, maybe that was it, only that's not what I'd call it.
Getz was a vampire."

"I'll accept that," Wolfe murmured.

"That's the way it was when I met Harry, but I didn't
know it until we were married, two years ago. I admit Getz
might not have got killed if it hadn't been for me. When
I found out how it was I tried to talk sense into Harry. I
told him his name had been connected with Dazzle Dan
so long that Getz would have to give him a bigger share,
at least half, if he demanded it. He claimed he tried, but
he just wasn't man enough. I told him his name was so
well known that he could cut loose and start another one
on his own, but he wasn't man enough for that either. He's
not a man, he's a worm. I didn't let up. I kept after him, I
admit that. I'll admit it on the witness stand if I have to.
And I admit I didn't know him as well as I thought I did.
I didn't know there was any danger of making him desperate enough to commit murder. I didn't know he had it
in him. Of course he'll break down, but if he says I knew
that he had decided to kill Getz I'll have to deny it because it's not true. I didn't."

Her husband was staring up at the back of her head, his
mouth hanging open.

"I see." Wolfe's voice was hard and cold. "First you plan

to put it on a stranger, Mr. Goodwin—indeed, two strangers, for I am in it too. That failing, you put it on your husband." He shook his head. "No, madam. Your silliest mistake was opening the window to kill the monkey, but there were others. Mr. Cramer?"

Cramer had to take only one step to get her arm.

"Good God!" Koven groaned.

Pat Lowell said to Wolfe in a thin sharp voice, "So this is what you worked me for."

She was a tough baby too, that girl.

Printed in the United States
by Baker & Taylor Publisher Services